Praise for Donna Clayton

"Donna Clayton pens a cozy romance
with a lot of humor, heart and passion."
—*Romantic Times*

* * *

Etienne suddenly realized that he was falling hopelessly in love with this woman.

Sighing, he closed his eyes and tried to relax. But the notions eddying in his head made that next to impossible.

All of these realizations posed a huge problem for him.

He'd gone out seeking a wife. A princess. As the successor to the Rhineland throne, he knew his parents fully expected him to fulfill that goal.

Yet here he was at the top of Byron Mountain after having run away in the night with a woman who had no title, no fortune, no lands…not even a social standing to offer him and his country.

Had he totally lost his mind?

Or just his heart…

* * *

Don't miss next month's installment of the ROYALLY WED: THE MISSING HEIR series—*A Princess in Waiting* by Carol Grace (SR#1588).

Dear Reader,

Have you started your spring cleaning yet? If not, we have a great motivational plan: For each chore you complete, reward yourself with one Silhouette Romance title! And with the standout selection we have this month, you'll be finished reorganizing closets, steaming carpets and cleaning behind the refrigerator in record time!

Take a much-deserved break with the exciting new ROYALLY WED: THE MISSING HEIR title, *In Pursuit of a Princess,* by Donna Clayton. The search for the missing St. Michel heir leads an undercover princess straight into the arms of a charming prince. Then escape with Diane Pershing's SOULMATES addition, *Cassie's Cowboy.* Could the dreamy hero from her daughter's bedtime stories be for real?

Lugged out and wiped down the patio furniture? Then you deserve a double treat with Cara Colter's *What Child Is This?* and Belinda Barnes's *Daddy's Double Due Date.* In Colter's tender tearjerker, a tiny stranger reunites a couple torn apart by tragedy. And in Barnes's warm romance, a bachelor who isn't the "cootchie-coo" type discovers he's about to have twins!

You're almost there! Once you've rounded up every last dust bunny, you're really going to need some fun. In Terry Essig's *Before You Get to Baby...* and Sharon De Vita's *A Family To Be,* childhood friends discover that love was always right next door. De Vita's series, SADDLE FALLS, moves back to Special Edition next month.

Even if you skip the spring cleaning this year, we hope you don't miss our books. We promise, this is one project you'll love doing.

Happy reading!

Mary-Theresa Hussey

Mary-Theresa Hussey
Senior Editor

In Pursuit of a Princess

DONNA CLAYTON

SILHOUETTE *Romance*®

Published by Silhouette Books

America's Publisher of Contemporary Romance

Special thanks and acknowledgment are given to Donna Clayton for her contribution to the ROYALLY WED: THE MISSING HEIR series.

In loving memory of Doris Montgomery,
my mom, my friend

SILHOUETTE BOOKS

ISBN 0-373-19582-6

IN PURSUIT OF A PRINCESS

This edition published by arrangement with Harlequin Books S.A.

Visit Silhouette at www.eHarlequin.com

Printed in U.S.A.

Books by Donna Clayton

Silhouette Romance

Mountain Laurel #720
Taking Love in Stride #781
Return of the Runaway Bride #999
Wife for a While #1039
Nanny and the Professor #1066
Fortune's Bride #1118
Daddy Down the Aisle #1162
**Miss Maxwell Becomes a Mom* #1211
**Nanny in the Nick of Time* #1217
**Beauty and the Bachelor Dad* #1223
†*The Stand-By Significant Other* #1284
†*Who's the Father of Jenny's Baby?* #1302
The Boss and the Beauty #1342
His Ten-Year-Old Secret #1373
Her Dream Come True #1399
Adopted Dad #1417
His Wild Young Bride #1441
***The Nanny Proposal* #1477
***The Doctor's Medicine Woman* #1483
***Rachel and the M.D.* #1489
Who Will Father My Baby? #1507
In Pursuit of a Princess #1582

Silhouette Books

The Coltons
Close Proximity

*The Single Daddy Club
†Mother & Child
**Single Doctor Dads

DONNA CLAYTON

is the recipient of the Diamond Author Award for Literary Achievement 2000, as well as two Holt Medallions. She became a writer through her love of reading. As a child, she marveled at her ability to travel the world, experience swashbuckling adventures and meet amazingly bold and daring people without ever leaving the shade of the huge oak in her very own backyard. She takes great pride in knowing that, through her work, she provides her readers the chance to indulge in some purely selfish romantic entertainment.

One of her favorite pastimes is traveling. Her other interests include walking, reading, visiting with friends, teaching Sunday school, cooking and baking, and she still collects cookbooks, too. In fact, her house is overrun with them.

Please write to Donna care of Silhouette Books. She'd love to hear from you!

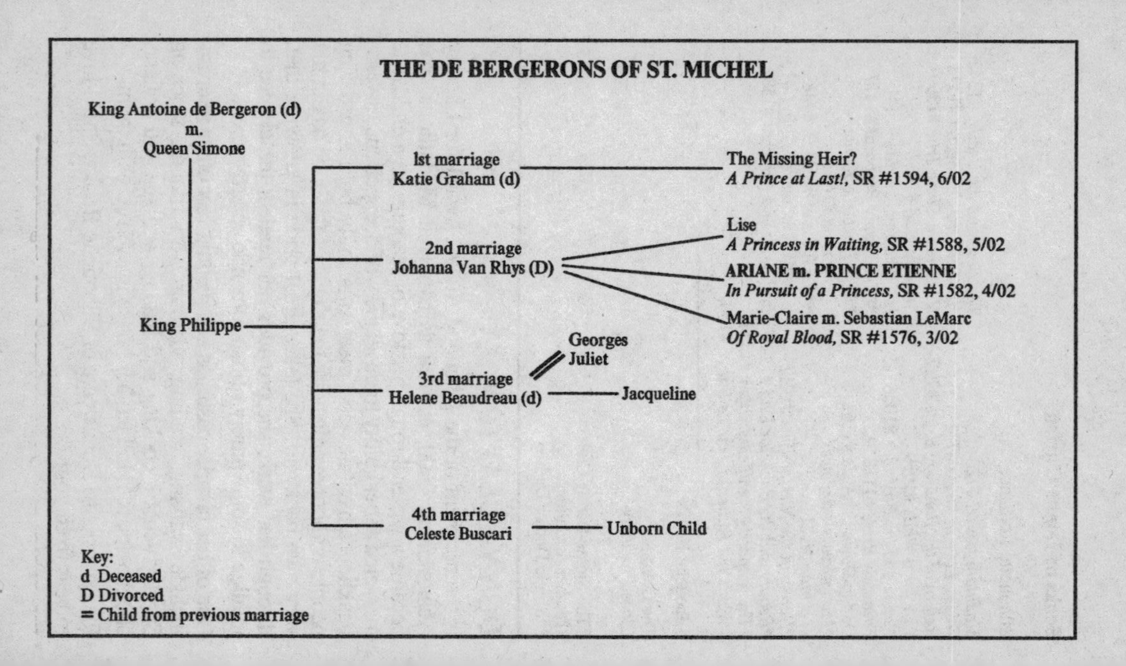
THE DE BERGERONS OF ST. MICHEL
King Antoine de Bergeron (d)
m.
Queen Simone
King Philippe
1st marriage
Katie Graham (d)
The Missing Heir?
A Prince at Last!, SR #1594, 6/02
2nd marriage
Johanna Van Rhys (D)
Lise
A Princess in Waiting, SR #1588, 5/02
ARIANE m. PRINCE ETIENNE
In Pursuit of a Princess, SR #1582, 4/02
Marie-Claire m. Sebastian LeMarc
Of Royal Blood, SR #1576, 3/02
3rd marriage
Helene Beaudreau (d)
Georges
Juliet
Jacqueline
4th marriage
Celeste Buscari
Unborn Child
Key:
d Deceased
D Divorced
= Child from previous marriage

Chapter One

"Let the mission begin." Princess Ariane de Bergeron glanced around, her heart pattering like the wings of a hummingbird as she made her way through the maze-like halls of the castle. Anyone overhearing her talking to herself would dub her a simpleton. But wasn't that just what she wanted? Let the citizens of this foreign country think she was silly. That fit her plans perfectly.

Yes, she was in a foreign land. And although the lush and hilly terrain of Rhineland was nearly as beautiful as her own neighboring country, she had to remember there were enemies here. Enemies who were plotting to seize her beloved St. Michel.

Ariane was so concerned for her countrymen, in fact, that she was here under the guise of responding to the interest of Prince Etienne Kroninberg. Just a little over six months ago, the prince had traveled to St. Michel to present her with a formal invitation to the opera. Everyone realized the significance of this visit. Etienne had clear intentions on Princess Ariane. And her father, King Philippe, had been in full agreement that the two royal families should unite.

Royal protocol had forced Ariane to accept the date, but if the truth were to be known, she found the opera to be the most boring pastime ever invented. And if the prince of Rhineland enjoyed opera, then he must be boring, as well. In order to entertain herself, she'd invited plenty of attendants and friends along for the evening. So many, in fact, that she'd spent little time alone with the prince. And if the complete truth were known regarding her conduct that evening, the crown prince would not only have been insulted, but downright outraged.

She grinned even now as she thought about her wicked behavior. The poor man. He'd obviously had no idea what he'd been up against. Now, had he invited her to go rock climbing or parasailing, maybe then she'd have wanted to get to know him. As it turned out, she returned to the opera house before the performance had ended...with Prince Etienne none the wiser, thank heavens.

However, it had been pure luck for her—and the whole of her country—that Etienne had shown an interest in her. Under the pretense of responding to his attention, she planned to keep her eyes and ears open, to collect all the information possible about who was plotting against her country.

As she descended the curved staircase, she glanced at the massive grandfather clock standing on the landing. Twelve minutes past the hour. Perfect. Ariane's grandmother, Dowager Queen Simone de Bergeron, had advised that when one was attending a party given in one's honor it was polite to arrive fashionably late, allowing time for the other guests to have assembled themselves.

Her name was announced and she paused inside the doorway of the ballroom as she'd been taught to do since she was a child. All eyes turned to her.

She was confident that her attire befitted her position. The soft silk of her strapless, form-fitting gown was the same midnight blue of her eyes. Her hair was swept off her shoulders with the perfect amount of wispy tendrils framing her face. The jewels in her tiara glittered, as did the diamonds gracing her earlobes and throat. Her father would have been proud....

Grief rushed over her, but she quelled the tears that so suddenly scalded the backs of her eyelids. Now was not the time to succumb to emotion, not with a room full of nobility scrutinizing her every move. Forcing her mouth to spread into a gracious smile, she made her way toward her host and hostess.

"Your Highness." Ariane greeted the king of Rhineland, offering the man a curtsy. But it was the queen who reached out to her.

"Oh, Ariane," the woman said, "we'll have none of that formal behavior from you. This is Giraud." She indicated her husband. "And I insist that you call me Laurette."

The king chuckled jovially. "You'll have to do as she says," he told Ariane. "I may wear the bigger crown, but Laurette runs the place."

They laughed, and Ariane was keenly aware of the fondness this couple obviously shared. All her instincts told her that she was going to like these people. She hoped she didn't discover they were involved in the conspiracy.

Laurette's expression turned somber. "I was so

sorry to hear about the passing of your father. King Philippe was a wonderful man.''

Sorrow welled up in Ariane. She had yet to come to grips with her grief. She smiled through the pain. ''Thank you. No one knew Father was having heart problems.''

''If there is anything we can do for you while you're here with us...''

The king's kind offer touched Ariane's heart.

Suddenly, Queen Laurette looked pained. ''I'll have to apologize for my son. I don't know what could be keeping him. He's always in some meeting or other.''

''I've sent out a search party.'' Giraud patted Ariane's arm. ''Don't worry. He'll turn up soon enough.''

''I'm sure he will.'' But even as Ariane stood there with her back to the crowd, she became cognizant of the low murmur rushing through the room. Surely the guests were discussing the prince's faux pas.

As she made her way across the polished marble floor, Ariane's smile didn't wilt in the least; however, she could feel annoyance spark inside her like the striking of a match. Of all the pompous, egotistical things for the prince to do! Arriving *after* her at a party given in her honor was not only arrogant, it was downright rude.

Like the loyal and trusted friend she was, Francie, Ariane's lady-in-waiting, stood nearby, the frown on her brow blatant proof of the aggravation she felt.

''He's an oaf to have done this to you,'' Francie said in a rush.

Ariane sighed, knowing exactly about whom Francie was speaking. "It's all right. I'm not concerned with the prince, anyway. You know that."

The words rolled off her tongue easily enough—and they *should* have been nothing but true. So why, she wondered, was she feeling so perturbed?

"Yes, but no one else here does," her friend reminded her. "And now everyone's talking. They'll all be thinking—"

"Keep your voice down." Ariane picked up a flute of champagne from a tray and nodded her appreciation to the servant who offered it. Once the man was out of earshot, she said to Francie, "I know what they'll be thinking—*and saying*. That I'm a desperate woman who is hankering after their prince."

Maybe that was the cause of her irritation. She didn't like being thought of as desperate.

"But *he* was the one who made first contact," her lady said, her ire obvious.

Francie got herself worked up easily and it never failed to tweak Ariane's humor. A grin curled the corners of her mouth. "It's going to be all right. Yes, I had hoped that my arrival would go smoothly, but I can surely handle a bumpy start." She smiled a genial greeting to an elderly man who strolled by. "Maybe the prince has taken ill. Or he's been detained with affairs of the state."

"At eight o'clock on a Saturday evening? Nothing could be more important to the prince of Rhineland than to be *here*." Francie's expression displayed her indignation as she firmly added, "Ten minutes ago."

"Okay, you've made your point. So the prince is an arrogant lout." Ariane sipped her champagne. "Speaking of affairs of the state...what do you say we find a likely candidate and talk politics? That *is* why I'm here."

Francie's nose wrinkled. "Political talk bores me. You know that."

Yes, Ariane did. "Then you go find a handsome man to dance with."

The woman started to go, but paused long enough to warn, "You be careful."

"Careful is my middle name. Besides—" Ariane let her eyes go wide with feigned naïveté "—as soon as I show them that I'm empty-headed and harmless, every official in the castle will be clamoring to impress me with all they know."

Etienne slipped into the ballroom using a side door. His parents would have his head for being late. But the matter couldn't be helped, he thought, his mouth firming into a grim line. He could only meet with the most trusted members of his Intelligence Service when everyone else was otherwise occupied.

Ruthless rumors were afloat. It had been reported to him that a person—or persons—within his father's cabinet wanted to seize control of the neighboring country of St. Michel. Etienne was appalled that someone wanted to take advantage of the de Bergeron family when they were still in mourning over the loss of King Philippe. The idea was barbaric in this day and age.

Granted, the unexpected death of the king left the country with no male heir—and it was common knowledge that the law of St. Michel declared that females could not rule. It was an archaic edict, but legally enforceable, nonetheless. No war would be fought. Not a single Rhineland soldier would march across St. Michel's border. This battle would be waged in the international courts. And all of this would take place in a civilized and peaceful manner. Yet it would be nonetheless barbaric in Etienne's mind.

He paused when he caught sight of his parents who were waltzing out on the dance floor. His mother was just getting over a serious bout of pneumonia. She'd been ill for some time now and his father had been worried that she may not recover completely. It was good to see them enjoying themselves.

He let his gaze travel slowly over the guests in the ballroom. It didn't take but an instant to find who he was looking for. She stood out in the crowd, his princess did. Ariane was that stunning. Heat spiraled like liquid smoke low in his gut.

Her honey-blond hair was twisted into an intricate coiffure, a few loose and softly curling strands falling to brush against her sexy bare shoulders whenever she moved her head. The line of her milky neck was long and graceful and delicate. She had the kind of throat that enticed a man to press his nose against warm skin, to inhale the distinct and subtle womanly aroma that would be hers and hers alone. Ariane, he silently surmised, would smell of sunny summer days and flowery meadows.

He had to admit, Princess Ariane's visit had him more than a bit perplexed. He'd made his intentions known prior to her father's passing. King Philippe had let Etienne know that he was quite in favor of a match between himself and Ariane. Etienne's own father was in favor of such an alliance as well. However, Princess Ariane hadn't seemed the least interested in Etienne as a suitor.

He'd returned home feeling rebuffed. He wasn't a quitter, though, by any means, and he'd had every intention of having another go at the beautiful Princess Ariane. However, his mother had taken ill, and Etienne had stood in for his father so he could be with his mother. Then King Philippe had died. Contacting Ariane during her time of mourning simply hadn't seemed appropriate.

No one had been more surprised than Etienne when the de Bergeron royal envoy had arrived announcing Princess Ariane's intentions of visiting Rhineland.

He started across the floor. Surely, the princess would be feeling affronted by his tardiness. He had some groveling to do. He may as well get it over with.

When he approached, all conversation stopped.

"Your Highness." He bowed deep, wanting to express his profound apology. He straightened, leveling his gaze on her beautiful deep blue eyes. "Please forgive me." He pressed a light kiss, first to one cheek, then the other, taking full advantage of the old-style traditional greeting. Her skin was warm satin against his lips. "I hope you believe me when I say my late arrival couldn't be avoided. I do apologize for my absence."

He'd been wrong. Her scent didn't bring to mind summer days and wildflowers. She smelled of starlit nights washed clean by fresh rain.

Her lovely gaze went round and she said, "You've been absent?"

The two men standing in the small group did their best to stifle the humor incited by the Princess's cutting question.

Touché, Etienne thought. He deserved that. She had every right to put him in his place.

Her smile was dazzling enough to steal away a man's thoughts.

"I've been having a wonderful conversation with the reverends here," she told him.

What she'd said took him aback. Surely the lords had introduced themselves. Unable to quell his surprise, he queried, "Reverends?"

"Yes," she said. "The pastors here were just telling me about your beautiful country."

"Princess," Etienne felt compelled to correct, "Lord Hecht is minister of the interior. One of his many duties includes suggesting policy for our parklands." The man named Hecht offered Ariane an indulgent smile. "And Lord Bartelow is deputy minister of trade. He advises the king on issues of commerce." When Ariane's gaze still didn't seem to register understanding, he allowed himself to go a little further. "These men have been appointed by my father to help him run our government."

Ariane's chuckle sounded like tiny bells as she focused her attention on the two elderly men. "Oh...and here I thought I'd been talking to men of the cloth. I heard the word 'minister' and...well, I just naturally assumed..."

Again, she laughed. Daintily. Infectiously. And although the lords politely joined her, Etienne could tell from the quick, covert expressions that passed between them what they were thinking: if brain cells were dynamite, the lovely princess apparently wouldn't have enough to blow her nose.

This exchange was Etienne's first inkling that something about the de Bergeron princess seemed...well, shifted just a little bit left of center. Her behavior was somehow...off. And as he stood there listening to her talk, this deviation from what he thought should be the norm became more and more pronounced. He wasn't too proud to admit that the situation had him highly perplexed.

At one point when Lord Hecht was explaining his plan to create more nature sanctuaries, Princess Ariane suddenly snagged a passing female guest by the arm and exclaimed, "I simply must know where you bought that dress. The fabric is heavenly."

The three men stood speechless at the sudden shift in the conversation. However, the women seemed happy enough discussing clothing designers.

As the evening progressed, Etienne became downright amazed at how the princess would ask seemingly coherent questions regarding someone's political position only to make a frivolous comment that left her looking, well, less than intelligent.

Etienne honestly didn't know what to think. Maybe Ariane wasn't the woman he'd believed her to be.

Being the crown prince of Rhineland, the one who would next succeed to the throne, Etienne had realized early in his life that he couldn't chose a wife purely on whim. For several years now, the king himself as well as the king's most trusted advisors had been discussing the subject of Etienne's taking a wife. No man liked the idea of others offering input on who he took as a life mate, but, well, that was just the way things were done when you were of royal blood. Especially so when you were in line to become king.

From what he'd learned of Ariane de Bergeron, he'd had high hopes that she could very well be the perfect woman for him.

She was poised, there was no doubt about that. Having this woman gracing his arm would make any man proud. She was most certainly beautiful. The kind of woman who stirred the most primitive instincts in a man. He was experiencing that just being near her now, he realized, feeling the embers of desire smoldering even as he stood next to her. She was of the royal de Bergeron bloodline, a stately and well-respected family. And he'd been told she was an educated woman, having studied in Switzerland, acquiring a degree in political science.

Several women had gathered round them now, and he frowned as he listened to the conversation at hand. Had Ariane just compared the running of a monarchy to shopping for shoes? This evening was becoming more bizarre by the moment.

Sources had informed him that the princess had a head on her shoulders...a head supposedly filled with an impressive brain. However, if he were to believe what he was seeing—and hearing—this evening he'd have to say there was nothing more than a big air bubble between her ears.

"Oh, my," Ariane exclaimed suddenly, "but it is warm in here, don't you think?" She batted her innocent eyes at Etienne, clearly expecting him to make all things right for her.

"If you'll excuse me for a moment—" he let his gaze touch upon hers and then glanced at the group at large "I'll have the doors opened and fetch a cool drink for the princess."

The women standing within earshot hid their smiles and the men's gazes slid awkwardly from his. Normally, it wasn't Etienne's place to do such menial tasks as seeing to the temperature of the room or arranging for guests' refreshment. On any ordinary evening, he would have handed the chore over to one of the servants who hovered nearby. However, with complete and utter bewilderment spinning his thoughts into a dozen different directions, this was turning out to be no ordinary evening he'd ever experienced.

He gave quick orders to push open the doors leading to the garden to the first servant he saw, then he scanned the room in search of someone carrying a tray of drinks. He stopped short when he caught sight of his mother looking wan, and he immediately made his way through the crowd toward her.

"Are you feeling all right, Mother?" he asked. "You look done in."

Her smile was tired. "I think I've just had too much fun this evening, is all."

"Where's Father? He should see you to your room." Etienne glanced around him. "Would you like me to escort you?"

"No, no." Laurette's brow puckered. "You go back to Princess Ariane. Are you seeing to it that she's having a good time? Have you asked her to dance?"

The queen's tone held a mild inflection of accusation and censure. Etienne couldn't stop the smile that spread across his mouth. "Yes, I've asked the princess to dance. So have half a dozen other men. However, so far she hasn't been so inclined to accept."

His mother looked utterly scandalized. "She *has* to dance. *With you.* What will everyone say? You see to it that you get that young woman out on the dance floor."

Dutifully, he said, "Yes, Mother." Then he gave her a small, teasing salute.

"Oh, now," she said, "stop that. I'm not trying to mother hen you. I just want—"

"I know exactly what you want," Etienne gently interrupted. "You want Princess Ariane's visit to go well. And so do I."

The elderly woman glanced toward the crowd that had gathered around Ariane at the far side of the ballroom. She murmured, "She's probably upset. If only you had been on time...."

"Mother, trust that I'll make everything right."

"You always do, dear."

Just then, Etienne's father joined them, reaching up to clap his son on the back.

"That's one beautiful woman who has come to Rhineland to see you, son," he told Etienne. "Don't let her get away."

Etienne grinned. "I don't plan to."

Well, he hadn't planned to. But after spending a couple of hours in her company, he wasn't so sure anymore.

"All my top advisors say she's self-assured, humorous and well-educated—"

From his father's opinion, Etienne could tell the man hadn't spent much time this evening in the princess's company.

"—and that she's just perfect for you."

Etienne remained silent, his mind churning with troubling thoughts.

Giraud's gray eyes softened as they leveled on his wife. "You'll have to see to things for the remainder of tonight's festivities, Etienne. I'm going to retire for the evening with my lovely wife. She might be feeling better, but I believe she's not fully recovered just yet."

This protective behavior warmed Etienne's heart. He hoped to someday make a match as loving as the one his parents shared.

That thought had his gaze drifting across the room until it latched onto Princess Ariane. The deep blue silk of her dress hugged the curves and valleys of her luscious figure. The soft light turned her blond hair to glistening honey.

"She's perfect," he softly murmured his father's opinion aloud.

Self-assured, humorous, well-educated. The description haunted Etienne's mind.

Something wasn't right here. All the information he'd been given pointed out the fact that things were not adding up. Ariane *was* all of those things, Etienne was sure. And if he was sure of that, then her behavior had to be some sort of put on.

He sighed. But that just made no sense to him. No sense at all.

However, for some odd reason, it seemed as though the princess wanted the people of his country to think she was naïve and...well, dim-witted. She was putting on a show. And quite a show it was, at that.

But the question was...for whom? And why?

Chapter Two

"As long as capitalism remains what it is," Rhineland's prime minister, Arvin Schmidt stated, "then surplus capital will never be utilized for the purpose of raising the standard of living of the masses in any country boasting free enterprise."

Oh, how Ariane desperately wanted to comment. She'd have loved to tell the man that capitalism was commodity production at the highest stage of development, when labor power itself becomes a commodity, and if it raised the standard of living it could not be capitalism because uneven development and wretched conditions were fundamental states where free enterprise reigned.

Arguing politics was her passion, but she bit her tongue and remained silent. Some of the silliness that had spewed from her mouth tonight had utterly mortified her. It seemed to her that she'd talked to everyone, and every person in the room must think that her brain was made of marshmallow fluff. She didn't like making herself look stupid, she was quickly learning. But it couldn't be helped. She needed the government officials to feel safe in expressing their political views in her presence. How else was she to learn who among them were working toward the annexation of her beloved St. Michel?

Just then Prime Minister Schmidt remarked, "There are rules to be followed for every form of government."

Something in the man's tone drew her attention as sharply as if she were zeroing in on a bull's-eye.

"No matter the type of leadership that rules," he continued smoothly, "laws *must* be followed. No matter how difficult that might prove for some citizens."

Was the man sending out a cryptic message? Ariane wondered. Or was he merely trying to impress her with his opinions. Keen interest buzzed through her veins like adrenaline and she allowed it to show on her face with the hope that Schmidt would elaborate a little more. However, before he could, she felt a light touch on her forearm.

"Pardon me, princess."

She turned to see Etienne, and she stared into his handsome face, realizing for the very first time the startling color of his eyes—pewter-gray. Fringed with dark lashes, the effect was enough to steal her breath away.

Ariane had been so miffed at the man earlier in the evening that she hadn't been able to control the urge to put him in his place. She had forced herself to ignore him when he'd first arrived, wanting to convey how insulting his tardiness had been to her. She'd focused the whole of her concentration on the two "ministers" she'd been talking to...she nearly grinned now as she thought of the complete genius of *that* sham. Surely after that silly assessment the prince and the lords thought her to be a total idiot.

But now her anger was gone as she really and truly saw Prince Etienne for the first time this evening.

She fumbled for words. Stumbled over her thoughts. And there wasn't a single ounce of deception or pretense in her behavior. She simply couldn't get her tongue and the notions in her head to properly jive. Something strange was taking place...it was as if she'd been a train barreling down a track and suddenly found herself completely derailed.

"May I have this dance?" he asked.

The wheels in her brain turned, but she couldn't seem to get her larynx to utter a single sound. He cupped her elbow in his palm, obviously expecting her to accept his invitation.

Panic welled up within her. No, no! she wanted to shout. It was bad enough that she'd made herself look stupid to the upper echelon of Rhineland society. She certainly didn't want everyone to discover that she also had two left feet!

It wasn't that she hadn't tried to learn to dance. She'd suffered through two full years of torturous dance classes. Although, the fact that the instructor had been a snooty little man who had made her feel nothing short of a lumbering elephant out on the dance floor when all her other siblings—full, step and half—had blossomed into elegant swans under the man's tutelage. And her stepbrother Georges, a man who hated to fail at anything, had finally thrown up his hands in utter frustration when he'd attempted to teach her.

With her heart pounding so hard that blood whooshed dizzyingly through her head, she was finally able to sputter, "C-can't you see I'm in the middle of a c-conversation with the prime minister?"

The question sounded abrupt even to her own ears, and Ariane was horrified that she hadn't tempered her tone.

Having been born a princess, Ariane had attended many balls and parties in her twenty-three years, and she'd become skilled at turning down invitations to dance. Her grandmother, Dowager Queen Simone, wanting to help her granddaughter work around this little problem, had trained her extensively on just how to decline a request to dance without hurting the feelings of the party offering the invitation. In fact, Ariane had succeeded in doing just that at least seven or eight times this evening.

But the way Etienne's dove-gray eyes sparkled had thrown her for a loop. Why hadn't she noticed before this moment how amazing—how mesmerizing—his gaze was?

The prince's grip on her elbow tightened gently but insistently, and he guided her away from the group. He murmured, "Our prime minister could talk the ears off a brass monkey. But I have orders from none other than the queen herself who threatened me if I didn't get you out on the dance floor."

The dread churning inside Ariane didn't abate a bit, but the humor playing around the handsome prince's mouth lulled her into querying, "And what did she threaten you with?"

Etienne chuckled, and Ariane could tell from the look on his face that this man was very fond of the woman who had given birth to him.

"Oh, she didn't specify the hazards I'd face if I didn't follow her instruction," he told her. "She didn't have to. She's been my mother for twenty-nine years. I know better than to disobey her wishes."

"Sounds like Queen Laurette is quite a tyrant," she teasingly surmised.

The prince grinned, and she felt as if the summer sun were shining full on her face.

He whispered conspiratorially, "Don't let this get about...but I've got my mother wrapped round my pinkie. However, I do like to keep her happy. So help me out here, would you? Just one little dance is all I need from you, and Mother's mind will be put to ease."

Maybe it was the fact that her own mom had died when she was seventeen, or maybe it was because she had such a terrible relationship with her current stepmother, the jealous and oh-so-insecure Queen Celeste, but Ariane found it very endearing, indeed, to discover that the prince had formed such an open and loving bond with his mother. And the fact that he didn't mind Ariane knowing how he felt about the queen, well, that was just icing on the cake.

The heels of her shoes clicked on the smooth marble floor that was fairly swarming with couples who had already begun swaying to the breezy orchestral melody.

She hesitated, then decided she'd better do what she could to warn him what he was in for. "Etienne, please..."

He stopped and looked down at her, apparent curiosity puckering his high, intelligent brow.

Oh. She'd made herself out to be foolish enough tonight, she hated the notion of divulging further faults. Finally, sheer desperation had her softly admitting, "I'm afraid I'm about to embarrass you."

Again, he chuckled and Ariane was bombarded with the sudden outrageous urge to place her palm against his chest to feel what she instinctively knew would be the sexy tremor of his laughter. Her eyes widened at the astonishing thought.

"You could never embarrass me," Etienne told her. "In fact, I'm sure I am already the envy of every man in the kingdom."

She knew he meant to flatter her with the compliment, but she was too anxiety-ridden to even smile at him. "You don't understand..."

Before she had time to explain, he whirled her around to face him, deftly snuggling one palm at the base of her spine, enveloping her hand in his free one.

The closeness of him, the heat of him, made her feel as if she were suddenly thrust into a vacuum from which she couldn't draw breath. Yet as soon as they began to move, she automatically craned her neck in an attempt to watch where she was going. She panicked at the thought of bumping into another couple, of stepping on his feet, of slipping on the smooth, polished marble. She imagined what a sight the two of them would make if they were to go tumbling to the floor. Her apprehension hitched up another notch.

Funny thing about the waltz, the leader was the one who moved forward. As long as she was stepping away from Etienne, she didn't think she'd mash his toes with hers. She could place her foot first and he was responsible for not trampling on her. However, the dance also involved a great deal of turning, and the very first time the prince guided her toward him every muscle in her body tensed up—and she planted her foot directly on top of his.

His handsome face registered more surprise than pain. Ariane chucked him a quick look of apology before dipping her chin to once more stare at her feet.

Etienne had been graced with the princess's regretful expression for only a moment, but the vulnerability he'd read in her eyes, on her furrowed brow, affected him in the most amazing manner. He felt this immense urge to soothe her turmoil, to protect her from the eyes and opinions that she feared, to sweep her away from the crowd…to ravage that perfect pink mouth of hers with fierce kisses.

Without another thought, he waltzed her right out the huge double doors and onto the flagstone veranda that overlooked the formal gardens. The music spilled out into the night right along with them, but they stopped dancing and walked in silence to the stone half wall that edged the area.

Moonlight washed across the trees and shrubs, dusting them in a soft, pallid radiance. The unusually warm spring had caused the flower bulbs to burst from the ground and send forth their heady scents. It seemed as though a million stars glittered against the velvety night sky.

"Thank you."

The gratitude in her sweet voice tugged at his heartstrings.

He couldn't keep the smile from curling the corners of his mouth. "How was it you missed Dancing 101?"

Etienne knew dance instruction was common practice for all children of royal lineage, so he was certain she'd understand his question.

Her sigh was as soft as the night air. ''Oh, I took the class,'' she admitted despondently. ''And I flunked it. Twice.'' She gazed up into his face. ''I thought the second time round I just might get a passing mark...but then I fell right on my behind during the last session of learning the foxtrot. After that, the instructor—a mean and unforgiving little man, I might add—refused to have me in his classroom.''

His grin widened, but Etienne turned his head away until he succeeded in snuffing out the chuckle that rose up in his throat. It was obvious that she felt bad enough about her plight without him laughing at her.

Keeping his expression just as straight as he could, he said, ''When is the last time you saw anyone dance the foxtrot?''

''That's the same thing I said to—''

She paused, seeming to realize the humor he found in her story.

''Okay,'' she told him. ''Go ahead and laugh. It *is* pretty funny.''

''Oh, no.'' He shook his head. ''I wouldn't dream of laughing at your expense.''

Her nose wrinkled, and Etienne thought it was the cutest thing he'd ever seen in his life.

''It's just that I have no rhythm,'' she complained.

He felt compelled to say, ''That's not it at all.''

Her perfectly arched brows lifted a fraction in silent question.

''It's the fear you have to conquer,'' he told her.

''Fear? Why, as far as I know, I'm not afraid of much of anything.''

Before full insult could set in, he rushed to further explain, ''It's clear to me that you don't trust your partner. You're afraid you're going to be led into disaster. The moment you realize that your partner is competent in his role, then your concerns will dissolve like sugar in water. Here, let me show you."

She balked, but he took her into his arms. Immediately, her spine arched and she stood tall, just as she'd been taught.

He settled his hand low on the curve of her spine, murmuring, "You have great form."

Great form, he wanted to repeat. He felt heated tendrils sprout and curl in the deepest depths of his gut.

When they were in position, her gaze unconsciously dipped downward.

"Oh, no," he softly chided. Tucking his bent knuckle gently under her chin, he tipped up her jaw. "Look me in the eyes. Relax. Don't even think about the steps. Don't give your feet—or mine—another thought. Just listen to the music. Let it roll through you. And trust me."

Iridescent moon rays cast half of her features in shadow. Her prominent features were highlighted by the pearly glow: cheekbone, brow, chin, nose. And what a perfect nose it was. Etienne had to force himself not to plant a quick kiss on its tip.

He gazed down into her beautiful face, their gazes locking...and something extraordinary happened.

"Trust me," he repeated in a whisper, pushing off into the first step of the dance.

The next few minutes seemed laced with magic. A mysterious je ne sais quoi that he'd never before experienced in his life. He couldn't tell if it was the silky night air, or the soft strain of the orchestra...or the gorgeous young woman who stared up into his face.

Her dark eyes never left his. Not for a second. And the atmosphere seemed to heat up with each step they took, each dip and sway and turn they made. They may have been under the open sky, but Etienne had the strange sense that time itself was drawing around them like a warm and protective blanket.

The waltz they performed on the stone terrace was nearly flawless. There could be no other way to describe it.

Finally, the music faded, and the two of them stood there in that dancers' stance seemingly hypnotized. She studied his face as if she was seeing him for the very first time. The heat of her penetrated the silk of her dress, and he was sure his fingertips would be scorched. The muscles of her elegant, milky throat convulsed as she swallowed. Still they stood motionless, silent.

Of course, what seemed a hushed eternity couldn't have been more than the span of five or six heartbeats.

There was an intensity in the moment that called to Etienne. And it would have been so very easy for him to bend toward her. To place his lips against hers. To taste what he thought must be the delectable honeyed sweetness of her mouth.

But the part of his brain housing his common sense flickered to life. Doubts about this woman flooded into his thoughts. He was certain she'd been playacting all night. Pretending to be something she was not. And he couldn't help but wonder why.

In the end, he released her, clasping his hands behind his back so as not to surrender to the overwhelming desire he felt to kiss her, to touch her.

When he released her, she blinked slowly, once, twice. There was a lethargic sleepiness in her expression, and Etienne got the feeling that she was waking from a trance. He knew exactly how she felt. Then he noticed that her chest rose and fell as if she were out of breath...or physically reacting to the high intensity of the moment. Heaven could attest to the fact that he certainly was.

"I can't believe it."

The awe expressed on her face only made her all the more beautiful.

"I can't believe I waltzed without crushing your toes."

Her chuckle was filled with both giddiness and delight, and Etienne had to make a conscious effort not to reach out to her, then and there.

"Dancing won't ever be my favorite pastime," she remarked. "But at least now I know I can do it." Seemingly without thought, she added, "With the right partner, of course."

Her aside only seemed to heighten the thick atmosphere that swirled around them in the night air. He couldn't help wondering if she was as conscious of it as he was.

"I-I'm suddenly feeling exhausted," she whispered abruptly. "I hope you'll forgive me if I bid you goodnight."

He nodded a single, silent farewell, but she strode away from him so quickly that he doubted she even saw it.

The rusty quality of her voice coupled with the blatant fact that she was so obviously fleeing the scene told him that—yes—she had realized the magic that the two of them had conjured in those short few minutes under the stars.

* * *

Ariane came awake slowly, stretching on the luxurious bedding like a languid kitten. Sunlight streamed into the airy room and the warbling of birds, muffled yet melodious, could be heard even though the windows were closed against the morning chill.

All through the night she'd been plagued with dreams of pewter-gray eyes so fiery that she'd become consumed by them, of an embrace so secure that it had robbed her of all thought, of skin so hot that she felt burned by its touch, of a jaw so strong it was mesmerizing, of a mouth so perfect and kissable that she'd become thoroughly obsessed by the idea of tasting—

Stop!

Opening her mouth, Ariane gulped in a head-clearing breath as she pressed her palm flat against the base of her throat. She didn't want to think about what had happened between Etienne and herself at the ball last night. And she certainly didn't want to dream about the man.

Okay, so they had shared a few minutes together out under the silky night sky.

A few surprising—no, *amazing*—minutes.

Ariane did all she could to ignore this more precise description of the time she'd spent on the terrace with the prince.

Her trip to Rhineland held a solitary purpose. To glean political information for the head of her country's security force, Luc Dumont, who had been none too happy that she'd insisted on coming on this mission. But insist she had. She must remember her goal. She must remember that Etienne was a convenient motive for her visit. That was all he was. She refused to allow him to become anything more than that.

To allow fanciful thoughts to frolic around in her head would be useless. She and Etienne would never—could never—be anything more than they already were—mere acquaintances.

And the reality of her life was the reason.

Not only remembering, but focusing on the practicality of this fact made it all that much easier to clear the sweet but hopeless dreams from her head.

Movement at the window drew her gaze, and Ariane smiled as she watched the goldfinch that sat on the deep stone sill. The bird searched and pecked, then sang a few resounding notes, then went back to searching and pecking.

It felt so nice to be away from the tension that had built up in her home back in St. Michel. Her stepmother, Celeste, had never been the easiest person to live with, and luckily the palace was big enough that avoiding the woman was quite easy. However, since King Philippe's death, the queen—as Celeste preferred to be called these days—had become downright cantankerous.

Granted, the woman was nearly seven months pregnant. And the stress over worrying about the gender of the child she carried was probably contributing to her ill humor.

Ariane turned over onto her side and adjusted the pillow under her head.

The only way for her stepmother to retain even a modicum of her power was if she gave birth to a boy. A male child who would be in line for the throne. Of course, Celeste had professed to have taken a test that proved the gender of her baby, but Ariane wasn't the only one in the palace who thought it strange that the queen had yet to produce the medical documents to confirm that fact.

Smoothing her hand over the soft Egyptian cotton spread, Ariane sighed.

Even if her stepmother bore a baby boy, that child might not be first in line to be the next king. That honor would go to the child conceived during the marriage of Philippe, then crown prince of St. Michel, and an American woman named Katie Graham.

The young couple had fallen madly in love when Philippe had been eighteen. They had married without their parents' consent, and because Katie had been under the legal age to do such a thing, Philippe's parents had tricked them into believing that their union was null and void, that their marriage certificate wasn't worth the paper it was written on.

Philippe's mother, Ariane's grandmother, Simone, had expressed a deep regret over her deceitful actions of all those years ago when she'd recently relayed the story. She'd told Ariane and her two full-blooded sisters, Lise and Marie-Claire, that she and her husband had only been acting in what they truly believed to be their son's best interest.

So all those years ago the young couple parted. Philippe resumed his education and the training he'd need to act as king, and young Katie had left St. Michel brokenhearted—*and pregnant.*

If the child Katie had delivered was male...and if he was still alive...then *he* would be the next de Bergeron king of St. Michel.

However, Simone had told them all that as far as she knew Philippe had never heard from Katie again.

And no one had any idea if the child the woman gave birth to was male or female.

What worried Ariane more than anything was the future of St. Michel. Hundreds of years ago, those wonderful, loving people had fought long and hard to form their own realm, for the right to pledge themselves to the de Bergeron family. Yet it seemed that keeping their country intact was hinging on the discovery of the whereabouts of one little baby, hopefully now a grown man.

The de Bergeron missing heir.

Ariane placed her fingertips to her mouth to stifle a yawn.

Of course this turn of events—this fantastic story brought to them by Simone—affected Ariane and her sisters. But the fact that her own parents' marriage had been invalidated and that Ariane and her sisters had been deemed illegitimate should have upset Ariane more than it did. She should be terribly distressed by the idea of having her title stripped from her, of losing her position in society. Ariane couldn't quite put her finger on why the notion didn't ruffle her more.

It could be that the calm she felt over her situation was possible because she knew no one but her sisters, her country's prime minister, close family members and Luc Dumont, the head of St. Michel's security force—trusted family members and friends, one and all—were privy to her and her siblings' predicament. Once the rest of the world learned of the fact that she was misbegotten, then it could be that she'd fall completely to pieces.

What would Prince Etienne think when he learned

the news? The question flitted unbidden through her head like a leaf tossed on the wind.

Ariane threw back the blanket and sat up on the edge of the mattress. She shoved the silly query from her mind. What did she care what he thought? What did she care what *anyone* thought?

A nice hot cup of tea was what she needed to clear away all these unpleasant doubts and questions.

The guest suite in the Kroninberg Palace was spacious and sunny. It consisted of two en suite bedrooms, one for her and one for her lady-in-waiting, connected by a delightful high-ceilinged sitting room. That's where she found Francie munching on a piece of buttered toast.

"What time is it?" Ariane asked, surprised to see that breakfast had been served on a large tray. "Shouldn't we be taking the meal with our hosts?"

"Everyone's sleeping in this morning." Francie wiped her fingers on the crisp, white linen napkin in her lap. "The maid told me when she delivered the tray, so I decided not to wake you."

Ariane poured a steaming cup of tea from the porcelain pot. "So how did you sleep?" she asked. After dropping in one sugar cube, she stirred and then eased herself down in the velvet armchair flanking Francie's.

"Just fine."

Her lady looked as if she were the proverbial cat that had swallowed a canary.

"Okay," Ariane said, "out with it. What's on your mind?"

"Oh, nothing."

Francie's voice had a sing-song quality to it that relayed that the opposite was the real truth of the matter.

"It's just that I watched you go outside with the

prince...and not too much later you came rushing back through the doors and right out of the room. Your face was flushed and you looked...well, you looked as if something had happened." She swept a few nonexistent crumbs from her lap. "When I followed you up here, you'd already shut yourself up in your bedroom. Which was a clear sign to me that you didn't want to talk about what happened. Which tells me that something *did* actually happen."

"You're deluding yourself, my friend." Ariane took a sip of her tea, but she was cognizant of the slight tremble of her fingers. The last thing she wanted to talk about was her time out on the terrace with Etienne. "Nothing happened. Nothing at all." When Francie's eyes rolled expressively, she reasserted, *"Nothing."*

Her friend chuckled. "What is that old saying? The one about the princess protesting too much? I think that just might fit you to a *T.*"

Ariane let her gaze settle on the ornate teacup and said nothing.

Evidently not getting the message that Ariane didn't want to discuss the matter, Francie boldly asked, "What did you talk about when you were with Etienne? And how come you rushed away from him and left the party?"

"You don't take a hint very well, do you?" Ariane quipped.

Just remembering those pewter eyes, and how she'd seemed to fall headfirst into them...Ariane's heart tripped an unsteady beat and she felt all shaky inside.

She had no idea what had happened to her during those moments. Etienne's arms had enveloped her securely. She'd become almost entranced by his steady gaze. The heat of him had swathed her like a warm and protective cloak. Somewhere in the back of her brain she's been aware that the spicy scent of his cologne held a hint of citrus. The combination had been utterly enticing.

Trust me.

Even now, the mere memory of his rich, resonant voice sent shivers coursing down her spine like a shower of cool spring rain.

She'd been enraptured. By his gaze. His scent. His touch. By *him.*

Never before had she been so stirred by another human being.

When Ariane failed to rise to Francie's bait, the woman remarked, "Etienne is awfully handsome."

She waited, and Ariane remained stubbornly silent.

"He looked awesome last night."

More silence.

Finally, Francie blurted, "And those trousers he wore accentuated his nice, tight butt, too."

Ariane gasped, tea splashing over the rim of the cup. "Francie!"

Her friend giggled. "Well, I'm glad to see you're alive and well. With all the silent treatment I'd thought you'd died right where you sat."

Sighing, Ariane pursed her lips for a moment. Then she said, "I am alive and well. And I agree with everything you just said. The prince is a handsome man. And he looked delectable last night." She grinned. "And I did notice his butt. Are you happy now that I've bared my soul?"

Francie grinned with clear delight.

Then Ariane's shoulders drooped a fraction and she lifted her chin determinedly. "But tell me something...what is the fabulous prince going to say once he learns that I'm no longer a princess?''

The pleasure slowly slid from Francie's expression.

''I'm here on a mission,'' Ariane continued firmly. ''I'm on an assignment that just might help our countrymen. *That's* what I have to focus on.''

Francie looked contrite. ''Yes, but there was no royal proclamation that said you couldn't have a little fun while you're here.''

Ariane shook her head in disagreement. ''That kind of fun will only lead to hurt and heartache. For everyone involved.''

Chapter Three

Etienne sat at the end of the long table, making a great effort to appear interested in the story being recounted by the man sitting next to him. No matter how hard he tried, he simply couldn't seem to spark an interest in the gentleman's escapades of starting a coffee bean plantation in Kenya. In fact, it was all he could do not to doze off into his raspberry sorbet.

It could have been because the man's adventure had taken place nearly a half century ago, or that he kept losing track of the storyline which caused him to repeat some portions of the tale several times over. Still, Etienne did his best to chuckle at all the right places and raise his brows to show he was impressed when the exploits required it.

All through dinner, though, his gaze kept skimming down to the other end of the table where Ariane sat at his father's left. For the past several evenings Kroninberg Palace had been a hive of activity. First had been the ball welcoming Ariane to Rhineland. Then for three nights running, the formal dining room had been filled with government officials, dignitaries and special friends of the family who wanted to spend some time with the princess.

Etienne would have given his eyeteeth to have been seated next to Ariane. But since she was the guest of honor, her place was near his parents. And as a member of the Kroninberg family, Etienne had to do his part by sitting at the opposite end of the table and entertaining the guests who were not fortunate enough to sit nearer the princess.

During each lingering meal, Etienne had had a hard time giving the dinner guests his full attention. And the reason was simple.

Ariane.

Tonight she wore a sleeveless, figure-hugging dress in a captivating shade of burnt orange. The hue of the shiny-looking fabric set off both her deep blue eyes and her tanned, curvy body. Her honey-blond hair fell, sleek and loose, just past her shoulders, and Etienne kept daydreaming about combing his fingers through those soft tresses.

Ariane's easy smile flashed now at something his mother said, and he felt as if someone had stirred a pile of slow-burning embers inside him. Heat coiled in his belly and his jaw unwittingly tightened against the yearning that was kindled.

He wanted this woman. In the worst way.

Etienne still suspected she was playacting. That the empty-headed persona she was presenting was just that. A mask. A guise.

However, he had to admit that he wasn't quite sure. If she was putting on a show, she sure was good at it. Not once in the days that she'd been in Rhineland had she slipped up. Time and again, she'd draw the government officials into political discussions only to make some outlandish remark that made her seem downright silly.

But why did she continue to choose a topic on which she seemed to know so little? Did she not realize how dense it made her appear? Maybe she really *was* flighty and shallow.

No. Etienne refused to fall for that, no matter how hard the princess was working to make everyone around her believe it. There was an intelligence in those midnight eyes of hers that just seemed to be screaming for release.

What he needed to do was force her to show her true self. To somehow trip her up. And he didn't want to do that in the company of anyone else.

Suddenly a plan formed in his head. He'd invite her to dinner in his private suite, talk to her about world governments. She certainly seemed interested in the subject. He'd make some purposefully erroneous remarks about different political principles and then he'd see if she rose to the bait. He nearly chuckled at the perfection of his plan. No woman could resist correcting a man who was blatantly wrong. Ariane would be no exception.

But what to do about the princess's lady-in-waiting? Simple good manners dictated that he invite Francie along to dinner, too.

Then he thought of Harry, his equerry. The two of them were close friends…Etienne suppressed a grin…they'd even been partners in crime a time or two when they'd been students together at Eton. Berkshire, England hadn't known what had hit it after the two of them had pulled a couple of their harmless pranks.

His friendship with Harry had been what had prompted Etienne to ask the Brit to move to Rhineland as his personal assistant.

Harry's ornery streak was still thick enough that he could easily come up with a scheme to coax Francie out of Etienne's apartments, leaving Etienne alone with Ariane for a while. Better yet, Harry could waylay Francie even before the two women were to arrive for dinner.

Etienne could hardly contain his mirth as he realized that his own ornery streak hadn't faded much over the years.

The plan set, he nodded enthusiastically at something the old gentleman beside him said, and when everyone around him laughed, he followed suit. However his mind was focused on tomorrow evening…when he'd succeed in getting Ariane alone.

Where in the world was Francie? Ariane paced the sitting room of the guest suite. She'd been dressed and ready for half an hour.

Dinner with the prince. In his apartments.

Ariane trembled inside.

Her case of nerves had a twofold cause. First off, she was uneasy about her ability to keep up this brainless façade. So many times over the past few days she'd nearly blurted out her true opinions to the administrators and bureaucrats she'd talked with. She'd discovered just how much she abhorred looking like a senseless idiot.

And secondly, she'd done everything she could to keep from being alone with Etienne. Those mesmerizing moments they had shared on her first night in his country had really thrown her for a loop.

Before arriving in Rhineland she'd thought of Etienne as nothing more than a means to an end in her goal of discovering who was plotting against her country. But she'd quickly discovered that the prince was an alluring man. A sexy danger to her mission. Like flint against steel, he sparked feelings in her that she wasn't up to dealing with right now.

When she'd received his dinner invitation this morning, her first reaction had been relief. All those formal meals were beginning to get to her. She'd smiled so much that her cheek muscles were becoming sore.

Fretfulness had Ariane actually opening the door of the guest suite and peering down the hallway one way, then the other, in search of Francie. She stepped back inside and shut the door.

She glanced at the beautifully carved German cuckoo clock on the wall. Being fashionably late was one thing, but this was bordering on nothing short of bad manners.

What was worse? she wondered. A terribly tardy arrival? Or visiting the prince's private apartments without her lady in tow?

Certainly, Etienne would have staff members in attendance to serve the meal. And surely Harry, his personal assistant, would be present, as well. There should be plenty of people milling about to act as chaperones.

Not that a princess needed a chaperone in this day and age. However, Ariane almost smiled as she thought of how her elderly and quite conservative grandmother, the dowager queen, would respond. It was never seemly, Simone would say, for a single woman to visit a bachelor's private rooms unescorted.

Finally, with a frustrated sigh Ariane decided she could wait no longer. She took a final look at herself in the full-length mirror, giving a small nod at the thought that her black trousers and apple-green sweater fit the casual dress requirements stipulated for tonight's date.

Adrenaline surged through her. This was not a *date,* she silently chided herself. She had simply accepted an invitation for dinner. She had to eat, didn't she? And so did the prince. They were simply going to share a meal together. That was all.

She'd told Francie the honest to goodness truth about her feelings regarding her chances of a real relationship with the prince. The man wouldn't be interested in her in the least once he found out that she'd lost her title. Dabbling in the allure he stirred in her would be fruitless. And wrong.

She was smarter than that.

The center of the hallway leading to Etienne's suites was covered with a plush peach-colored carpet that muffled the sound of her steps. Like all the other doors in the palace, his was massive and constructed of some dark, rich wood that glowed with an aged patina that only hundreds of years could produce.

She knocked, and the door was opened almost automatically by none other than the prince himself.

"Good evening," he greeted. "I was beginning to think you weren't coming."

"I'm sorry. I was waiting for Francie, but she never did show up." She entered the room, impressed by its masculine design. The furniture was oversized and upholstered in leather. The color scheme was dove-gray and burgundy. It was easy to conclude that the masculine furnishings fit Etienne.

"Why, she's with Harry," he said easily. "I thought you knew."

"No, I didn't." Ariane frowned. "Francie's usually very good about keeping me informed on such matters."

Etienne lifted one shoulder. "Harry told me he invited Francie riding."

Now she was really confused. "But she's afraid of horses."

He grinned. "That's what Harry said. And he was appalled by the idea. He talked Francie into letting him give her a riding lesson."

His smile quirked up one corner of his mouth, and Ariane's knees went weak at the sexy sight.

Etienne raised his dark brows. "Harry has a way with women."

She blinked, shaking her head, and she couldn't stop herself from smiling. "He must." Almost to herself, she murmured, "I can't imagine Francie going within twenty yards of a horse, let alone sitting in a saddle."

"I hope you don't mind their missing dinner."

He led the way further into the room. Ariane followed.

"Have a seat—" he indicated the ornately carved table in the dining area just off the living room "—and I'll go ahead and plate up the food."

She made her way to one of the chairs, taking in the covered silver servers sitting on the sideboard. "You're going to serve?"

He nodded even though his back was to her as he uncovered the first silver server. "That's okay, isn't it?'' he asked, steam wafting heavenward. ''With Harry and Francie busy, I thought I'd take advantage of this...privacy. I had the meal delivered and told the maid she could have the evening off.'' He paused long enough to look at her over his shoulder. ''What better way for us to get to know one another?''

Something danced in his pewter gaze. Something she couldn't quite make out. Was that a teasing glint? Or something more serious? Before she could decide he pivoted back to the sideboard and reached for a soup bowl.

Ariane listened, suddenly aware of how very quiet the apartments were. No maid. No Harry. No Francie. The two of them were truly alone.

Her already jittery nerves became positively frayed at the ends. Pointing out that it wasn't proper for them to be alone in his quarters might please her grandmother to no end, but it would make Ariane look like an old-fashioned stick-in-the-mud.

Her gaze settled on his broad shoulders and the play of hard muscle and sinew under his soft cotton shirt as he ladled out the soup. Her mouth watered and she swallowed, blaming her overactive salivary glands on the delicious and distinct scent of the lobster bisque rather than the delectable sight of Etienne's toned body. Her gaze slipped lower, even. To the taut derrière that she and Francie both had complimented not so very long ago. And that's when he chose to turn around and face her.

While he carried the soup to the table, Ariane frantically avoided his gaze by focusing on unfolding her napkin and fumbling to place it in her lap.

''Thank you,'' she murmured as he set the bowl before her.

The bisque was creamy, and it should have tasted luscious on her tongue, but Ariane was too antsy to take much note of it. Etienne sat across from her. He'd lighted a set of three short, chunky candles and the flames flickered and danced, reflecting in his intense gray gaze.

They made small talk over the roasted capon with sage dressing and braised endive. He told her a little of his childhood. How the king and queen hadn't let their royal duties keep them from being loving parents who were very much hands-on with their son. Whenever possible they had taken their evening meal together. They'd attended his school functions, cricket matches and riding events. They had vacationed several times a year as a family.

Ariane thought Etienne's upbringing sounded picture-perfect. Just what she wanted for her own children...were she to have any, that was. She was too embarrassed to talk about her own youth. What in the world would she say? That her family was nothing short of dysfunctional? That her own parents had divorced when she was only three years old, and that her jet-setting mother hadn't really seemed to mind all that much about leaving her children behind? That the only "mother" Ariane really remembered was a nanny who had left the palace as soon as her ward had turned sixteen? That her father had married twice more over the years in some warped attempt to sire a boy child who would inherit the throne of St. Michel? That her current stepmother, her father's pregnant widow, could barely stand the other children her husband had fathered during his previous marriages? That the tension in the palace since the king's death often bordered on explosive?

She stifled a mournful sigh. For some odd reason, she didn't want Etienne to know just how off-the-wall her family situation was, or just how abnormal her upbringing had been.

It wasn't as if she hadn't been loved. Even though her father was very concerned with producing a male heir to inherit his kingdom, he'd loved his daughters very much. Showered them with attention when his duties had allowed it. Whatever parental affection she lacked had been made up for in the tight-knit bond of devotion she and her sisters had formed. And she felt close enough to Georges and Juliet, her father's second—actually, third—wife's children from a previous marriage, to be able to warmly call them her brother and sister. And twelve-year-old Jacqueline, Ariane's half sister, was the light of her life.

It was her father's fourth wife, Celeste, who had become the dark cloud hanging over the palace these days. The woman was just—

Ariane forced the shadowy thought from her head. She didn't want to spend time contemplating such unpleasantness.

Dabbing her napkin to the corners of her mouth, she smiled at the prince. "Dinner was wonderful."

"Marjorie will be happy to hear that," Etienne said. "But then I knew she'd outdo herself. She studied at all the best French culinary schools. She's been with us for as long as I can remember. She's getting up there in years and does more supervising in the kitchen rather than cooking these days, but she told me she prepared this meal with her own hands."

"She must be very fond of you."

"And I of her."

A light sparkled in his eye, telling Ariane just how

much he liked the elderly woman who ran the Kroninberg Palace kitchen.

Her shoulders drooped a fraction and her gaze slid from his as the place she called home once again failed dismally in comparison. With Celeste in charge of running the de Bergeron household, staff never seemed to stay for very long. It was impossible for Ariane or anyone else in the family to strike up the kind of affectionate relationship that Etienne obviously shared with Marjorie.

"Let's take our coffee out on the patio," Etienne suggested.

He rounded the table and helped her from her chair. He had exceptional manners. She'd expect nothing less from a noble, yet his attentive behavior made her feel very…special. The scent of his cologne, an enticing mix of warm spice and citrus, swirled on the air, and she fought the urge to close her eyes and savor it in a deep inhalation.

She paused at the set of French doors while he went to the sideboard to pour two cups of coffee.

"I noticed," he said when he came toward her and handed her a cup, "that you haven't said much about your family."

Ariane murmured, "I haven't, have I."

The soles of her shoes grated softly against the ancient stone underfoot that had been worn smooth and shiny with time. The fragrance of lilac hung, ripe and heavy, in the silky night air.

"You warm enough?"

His query was automatic, and his concern for her made her insides grow snug and cozy with appreciation. She'd thought the man would be boring…stuffy, even, but she was learning that he was very caring. And he stirred something in her. Something mysterious. Exciting.

"I'm fine, thank you," she said.

He sipped his coffee, and Ariane wondered what it might be like to taste the rich liquid that glistened on his moist, full bottom lip. The unbidden thought made her start. Immediately, her gaze flew to the cup and saucer she held and she was relieved to find that she hadn't sloshed any coffee over the rim.

"I guess it's hard for you to talk about it," he said. "Your family, I mean. It must be terribly hard. Mourning the loss of your father."

His mention of her bereavement had tears springing to her eyes. She missed her father. Terribly. Pined for his laugh. His loving smile. She missed the attention he used to bestow on her and her sisters. Albeit, the attention he gave them was sporadic—he did have a country to run—but when he came to the playroom to visit them, they always had a lovely time together.

He'd been a good man. A shrewd and judicious ruler. The country had prospered under his reign. The people of St. Michel had respected Philippe de Bergeron. Ariane could always be proud that he had developed such a good reputation among his people.

However, it hadn't been the grief she suffered over her father's sudden passing that had kept her from talking about her family, about her childhood. It had been fear of humiliation. Pure and simple. She didn't want Etienne comparing her motherless upbringing to the ideal childhood he'd experienced. No way, no how.

"You know," Etienne said, "I've been thinking about the changes I'll make when I become king of Rhineland."

She was both surprised and relieved at this abrupt and unexpected change of topics.

"Changes? You think your father's ruling philosophy needs amending?" Her curiosity piqued, she turned to face him fully.

Moonlight turned his thick head of hair to a rich chestnut and his angular jaw threw a shadow across his corded neck. She knew if she were to run her fingertips down the length of his throat that his skin would be hot to the touch.

The thought was so vivid that she automatically tightened her hold on the coffee cup to make certain she hadn't acted on the notion. A hemmed-in feeling began to creep over her. Ariane desperately tried to shrug off the odd sensation and focused on the interesting conversation at hand. Etienne might be about to give her some great clues regarding who might be plotting to annex her country. She'd best pay strict attention.

"I'm thinking it's time for a hike in taxes," he stated boldly. "But I haven't decided if I should implement a luxury tax—" he grinned "—demand a levy on the toys bought by my richest citizens. Or apply a smaller tax that will affect the middle-class populace."

What he said surprised her to such a degree that she set down her cup and saucer on the nearby glass-topped table.

"Why?" she asked. "Rhineland's economy is very stable. And has been for years."

"I equate stable with stagnant. We haven't had a tax increase since my grandfather's reign. Change for the pure sake of change could be a good thing."

"It could be a bad thing, too." A stupid thing, was

what she really wanted to say. "You couldn't impose a tax increase without the backing of your officials, and without a solid reason to back up your proposal, I don't see how you'll get them to agree."

A strange expression lit his gaze, but before Ariane could come to terms with what it might mean, he turned his head and looked out over the vast manicured lawns.

Softly, he said, "Who was it who said, *'L'etat, c'est moi'?*"

"I am the state," Ariane repeated. Without thought, she added, "Louis the XIV coined that phrase. But he was an oppressive tyrant."

Etienne nodded, grinning slyly. The look should have set off warning bells in her brain, but she was too concerned with the unsuspecting citizens of Rhineland to notice.

"Ever heard of the divine right of kings?" he asked.

She nearly snorted, but thankfully suppressed the reaction. "You don't honestly believe that sovereigns are direct representatives of God, do you?" Derision laced the edges of her tone. "That's ancient doctrine. And if you remember, it's what led to the French Revolution. No one in their right mind would consider—"

Her jaw snapped shut as she realized just how far down the path of this intellectual conversation Etienne had led her. Her gaze caught and held his, and she saw that odd expression...that dancing light...flashing humorously in his cool gray eyes.

Hoping to cover her blunder, she chuckled with as much delight as she could muster. "You're teasing me.'' She let her chin dip and she shot him a coy look. ''You ought to be ashamed.''

Now her mind worked frantically. Could she salvage the situation? What could she say to make herself look less erudite? She shouldn't have reacted so rashly to his insinuation that he intended to govern under autocratic rule, but she'd become so riled at the suggestion that he intended to take advantage of his own subjects that she hadn't thought before speaking her mind.

Marshaling a serious tone, she proclaimed, ''But I'd think that the woman you take as your wife...the queen of your country...would *love* the idea of a tax hike.'' She smiled prettily. ''It would mean more money for jewelry and ball gowns and shoes. A queen can never have enough shoes, you know.''

She was breathless as she waited to see if he fell for her ploy, yet at the same time she felt utterly mortified to think that he might. Appearing so darned superficial galled her to no end.

Etienne set his cup down next to hers and approached her. His gaze was as silvery as the moonlight. Enthralling. The night air seemed to heat up and swirl slowly, sensuously around the two of them.

''Now that you've brought up the subject,'' he said smoothly. ''Let's talk about who I might take as my queen.''

The sumptuous tone of his voice stunned all thought from her head.

''I'm so happy that we're finally alone,'' he continued.

His whispered words sent a shiver coursing across every inch of her skin.

"I'm so happy that you've come to visit Rhineland." He clarified, "To visit *me.*"

He ran the backs of his fingers down her jawline, then traced her bottom lip with the pad of his thumb.

She couldn't seem to pull her gaze from his, and she anticipated that if he were to press his lips to hers, his kiss would be laced with the flavor of rich French roasted coffee. She'd have given her best diamond tiara to taste what she guessed would be a most luscious experience.

Oh, heaven help her. Ariane felt sluggish. Drugged with the sudden desire that welled up like tidal water, filling ever nook and cranny of her being. Threatening to drown her. What a wonderful way to go!

But her self-preserving instinct had her fighting the fog that enveloped her brain. She could offer up a silent prayer, but she knew no deity would come to her aid. No angels were going to swoop down to save her. If she was going to be rescued from this thick, sensual air Etienne had conjured with his mere nearness, his gentle touch, she'd have to be the one to do it.

Think, Ariane. Think. The silent order was firm and it resonated through her head.

All this mannerly attention and romantic interest could be a strategy meant to lull her into a false sense of security. Etienne could be the person leading the faction of his government that wanted to seize St. Michel. If that were so, that made him the enemy! If that were so, it also made him an arrogant conniver!

Planting her palm firmly against his chest, Ariane dragged a lungful of head-clearing air into her body. She stepped away from him.

"I-I'm not feeling well all of a sudden," she blatantly lied. "I've come down with a terrible headache."

His expression was a strange mixture of concern and...was that *triumph?* But that made no sense. Her brain was whirling with too many overwhelming thoughts to figure out what he might be thinking. This entire evening had her dizzy with confusion.

All she could think about right now was getting away from this situation. Away from those silvery eyes. Away from the heat of him. Away from the desire that pulsed in her. Throbbed through her veins.

She turned from him. "I need to go to my rooms and lie down."

"Wait," he said. "I'll be happy to walk you back—"

"No!" Ariane hurried through the French doors. "I'll be fine. I know the way. All I need is a rest, I'm sure."

She rushed through the sitting room and out the front door of his apartments.

Etienne stood on the patio staring out at the night, seeing nothing, his mind, his every thought on his beautiful princess.

He couldn't stop the chuckle that rumbled to the surface. He'd chosen the right bait to catch her when he'd suggested taking unfair advantage of his people. She'd been clearly incensed by the idea. And when he inferred that he planned to make Rhineland an autocratic monarchy with that mention of the divine right of kings, she'd fallen for the lure—hook, line and sinker—and he'd reeled her in.

And what a catch she was! His grin widened further and he felt a tug of desire pull at his insides.

Oh, she'd tried to salvage her ruse. But she'd nearly choked on her ditsy comment about higher taxes affording a queen more material wealth. She loathed looking like the village idiot. Realizing that amused Etienne immensely.

He wasn't the kind of man who liked to play games with people. But he felt justified in the laying of this trap for Ariane because it was so obvious to him now that she *was* playacting. In reality, she was an intelligent woman with quite a head on her shoulders. Especially where politics was concerned. And the inanity she'd been presenting to all and sundry was just a mask she wore.

This realization had his curiosity working overtime. Why on earth would she want everyone to believe she was brainless? he wondered for what felt like the thousandth time.

Before he could come up with a guess to the question, he was overwhelmed with an amazing sense of relief. He was delighted to learn that she was, indeed, an intelligent woman. For he feared that the lovely Ariane had stolen his heart. And no man wanted to think he'd fallen in love with a twit.

Chapter Four

Ariane pushed the brush through her hair, and once it was smooth and tangle-free, she made neat parts and began plaiting the strands. Francie was more adept at making a French braid than she was, but her friend had found something much more interesting to occupy her time lately than acting as Ariane's lady-in-waiting. Not that Ariane minded. The whole point in taking Francie on as her lady was to afford her friend the chance to meet eligible and suitable young men. Francie came from an old and well-respected family. Marrying just anyone was out of the question.

It seemed Francie meant to explore the possibility of a relationship with Harry. The couple had spent a great deal of time together ever since he'd succeeded in persuading her to climb into a saddle last week. They'd had daily rides and taken driving excursions into the small nearby towns. Seemed that Francie didn't have time for Ariane all of a sudden.

Being on her own had left Ariane feeling panicked.

Since their arrival in Rhineland, Francie had been a great excuse for Ariane not to have to spend time alone with Etienne. But since Francie and Harry had become something of an item, Ariane had pretty much lost that excuse.

However, she continued to succeed in sidestepping the handsome prince. One day this past week, Queen Laurette had taken her on a tour of Rhineland's finest medical centers. Ariane had enjoyed the opportunity to visit the children's wards. On another day, King Giraud had insisted Ariane tour some of the country's vineyards. They had tasted various wines: Riesling, Pinot, Viognier, Chardonnay, and an Auslese that had proved to be deliciously sweet.

She had discovered that Etienne's father was so interested in his country's vinters that he visited them often, always bringing his very own tastevin. The small saucer-shaped cup was made of highly polished silver, its ridges and crevices allowing him to inspect the color and clarity of the wine. Ariane had enjoyed her outing with the king, and he'd evidently enjoyed it, too. The next morning he'd sent her a gift. Her very own silver tastevin.

Two days ago, Ariane had slipped from the palace, unnoticed, for a day of shopping, and yesterday she'd ridden all around the countryside on a docile mare she'd borrowed from the royal stables.

How could she keep herself busy today? What excuse could she come up with to—

Staring into the mirror now, she recognized the desperate look haunting her eyes. Her fingers fumbled suddenly and she let her arms relax at her sides, the braid she was working to create slipping into a loose mess as she was struck with a terrible realization.

She was expelling more time and energy *avoiding* Etienne than she was in gathering political information for the head of St. Michel's security force. Luc would be upset when he discovered that she'd found out almost nothing about who in Rhineland might be plotting against her country. Rhineland's prime minister delivered cryptic messages that seemed laced with hidden threats about government, laws and rules, and Ariane found that mighty suspicious. And she'd overheard an oil tycoon named Berg Dekker complaining about having to pay to dock his barges at St. Michel. But she'd learned nothing concrete about who might be behind the actual conspiracy or to what lengths the rogues were planning to go.

Why was it that evading the prince had taken precedence over fulfilling her royal mission?

Well, darn it, Etienne was too good-looking for common decency. And he stirred in her emotions and feelings that were most *in*decent. She'd only been alone with the man twice...and both times she'd been overtaken by some strange dazed-like stupor. She hadn't been able to draw breath. She hadn't been able to think straight. She hadn't been able to speak properly. And the urges that had tugged at her...driving her to act...well, in a manner that was *not* befitting her position.

All she wanted to do when she saw him was—

Her heart thudded and heat rose to flush her face as shocking thoughts bombarded both her brain and her body. However, she wasn't able to stem the devilish grin that pulled at the corners of her mouth.

She should be so ashamed at the wicked and wanton notions rolling around in her head.

"And what are you smiling at so early this morning?"

Ariane's gaze rounded as she caught site of Francie's reflection in the mirror. Her friend stood in the doorway of her bedroom, and Ariane had been so preoccupied with her naughty thoughts that she hadn't even heard the door of the guest suite open or close.

Grabbing up the hairbrush, Ariane busied her hands. "I might ask you the same thing," she said, hoping to put Francie off. "Your cheeks are full of color and your smile is a mile wide. What have you been up to this morning?"

It was clear that Francie had lost her heart, Ariane thought, because a woman in love was too easy to distract.

"I have never met a man quite like Harry."

Francie's words were spoken on a euphoric sigh as she approached Ariane.

"Here, let me do that," she said, taking the brush from Ariane's hand. Then her eyes misted over as she continued, "He makes me all tongue-tied, and when I'm with him I can't seem to breathe."

Ariane grew still. Weren't those the very thoughts she'd just had about her own reaction to Etienne?

Francie ran the brush distractedly through Ariane's hair. "Harry is sweet. And sensitive." She caught Ariane's gaze in the mirror and whispered, "Is it too soon to say I think I'm in love?"

Shocked, Ariane let her brows shoot toward the ceiling. "My first instinct is to say yes. Francie, you've known the man for a week."

"Oh, but what a week it's been."

With nimble fingers, Francie parted her hair and began to plait the strands, over and under. Ariane noticed the dazed look in her gaze—the same dazed look Ariane had been stricken with both times she'd been alone with Etienne. Could it be that she was falling in love with the prince?

No. No! She would not allow herself to think such silly thoughts.

How in the world could she fancy herself in love with the prince? She barely knew the man. People in love knew everything about one another. Favorite songs. Favorite foods. Favorite activities.

"Last night, Harry took me for a walk in the garden. He said it was the place he loved best in all of Rhineland. He said it reminded him of the countryside of England where he grew up. However, then he said that he'd never enjoyed it as much as he did with me. He brought a bottle of champagne." Francie giggled like a schoolgirl. When she continued, her tone was hushed. "He kissed me, Ariane. Under the moonlight." She sighed, and her voice was awe-filled as she added, "I've never experienced anything like it before in my life. It was so romantic. He is so romantic!"

She fastened the end of Ariane's braided hair. The poor woman looked utterly overwhelmed with emotion.

Ariane felt the need to speak her mind. "Are you sure he's...well...suitable? You don't want your parents finding fault with your choice."

A smug gleam twinkled in Francie's eye. "He's in line for a dukedom."

There was pride in her voice, Ariane could hear it. "He must not have much money if he's working for Etienne."

Francie waved off the thought. "My family has

enough money for the both of us. I'm not worried about that. Harry will charm Mother, and Father will love the idea of having a British duke in the family."

"But—"

"No more buts, Ariane." Francie plunked her fists on her hips. "I want you to be happy for me."

Ariane stood up and turned to face her friend. "Oh, Francie, if Harry makes you happy, then I'm delighted."

So why didn't she feel delighted? she silently wondered as she hugged Francie to her tightly. What was this sensation sitting in the pit of her belly like a brick?

Stifling a groan, Ariane finally recognized what it was.

Envy.

She was envious of Francie's good fortune.

Once it was discovered that she was no longer a princess, no man would have her. Not a duke. Not even a court jester.

And certainly not a prince.

"I'd better go down to breakfast," she told Francie. "I don't want to keep everyone waiting."

"I won't be down. Harry and I had breakfast in town." Her gaze glittered with excitement as she added, "And we plan to have lunch out. After we've visited some antique stores. Harry loves antiques."

Ariane smiled. She knew her friend was a fiend for antique furniture.

"You have fun," Ariane called as she left the suite.

Making her way down the stairs, she wondered if she'd ever find someone with whom she could explore commonalities. She wondered if she'd ever meet a man who loved the outdoors or who enjoyed adventurous activities as much as she did, herself.

The image of an intense gray gaze flashed, unbidden, in her mind.

Did Etienne love to feel the wind blowing through his hair? Did he get excited at the mere thought of taking a hot air balloon ride? Would he climb to the top of a mountain for the sole purpose of seeing if he could do it?

Ariane came to a dead stop on the stairs. When, exactly, had the nebulous ''man'' in her thoughts become Etienne?

Her inhalation was suddenly shaky. She had better be careful. There was no chance of a relationship between her and Etienne Kroninberg. No chance whatsoever.

He might find her attractive now—and he *did* desire her, just as much as she desired him, that had been clearly evident both times they had been alone—but as soon as he discovered that she had the stain of illegitimacy on her name, no amount of allure would be enough for him to continue pursuing her.

He was the crown prince of Rhineland. It was important for him to make a good marriage. One that brought respect, privilege and wealth to his royal house. Doing so was his honor-bound duty.

Chasing after a woman with no title, no social standing, no land, no money save a small personal trust fund, would be the last thing Etienne would do. In fact, she wouldn't be surprised if the man actually ran from the very sight of her once he discovered the truth.

The instant she stepped into the breakfast hall, Ariane knew something was amiss. The room was narrow, and nearly forty-five feet long, with huge windows that let in the sun and allowed a spectacular view of the formal gardens and the rolling hills of the Rhineland countryside in the distance.

During her visit here, she'd learned that King Giraud conducted most of the affairs of state in a set of offices located in the east wing of the palace, so it was not unusual to see some of his ministers, cabinet members and advisors sitting at the table or serving themselves from the vast array of delicious smelling food offered on several sideboards.

Everyone nodded at her in greeting, but not one of them offered her a smile. It was almost as if they had a difficult time meeting her gaze. Even the servants seemed to avert their eyes, giving her a wide berth as they carried their trays in and out of the room.

Ariane's steps slowed as her thoughts swirled like a tornado. What on earth was wrong with everyone? Had she somehow disgraced herself and the de Bergeron name by breaching etiquette in some way? Granted, she'd stayed away from the castle most of yesterday, but she'd sent word to the queen of her intentions. Had she missed some meeting? Had she forgotten some important invitation? What indiscretion had she made that would have everyone treating her as if she'd contracted the plague?

Holding her head high, Ariane walked straight for the regal couple who sat at the head of the table.

"Your Highness." She smiled at the king and dropped a small curtsy. The greeting was a tad formal for breakfast, Ariane realized, but she wanted Etienne's father to understand that if she'd hurt him or his wife in any way, if she'd somehow embarrassed herself, she wasn't above accepting responsibility and offering humble apology.

It was Queen Laurette who spoke. "How are you this morning, my dear?"

"I'm fine," she replied, observing that both of their expressions seemed taxed. "However, I couldn't help but notice..."

Letting the rest of her sentence fade into oblivion, Ariane glanced around the room, then back at the king and queen. "There seems to be a great deal of tension in the air," she said. "Is everything all right?"

She'd always heard that it was the silent seconds that took the longest to pass. Ariane discovered the truth in this. The awkward stillness seemed to echo off the walls. Giraud and Laurette were obviously uncomfortable about something.

The king's gaze slid to his tea cup, and when he looked at her again, there was a sadness in his eyes that had Ariane's heart hammering in her chest. He had something to say, that much was clear. And it was obvious to her that he was trying valiantly to find the right words to speak his mind.

Bustling movement had all heads turning toward the door at the far end of the room where Ariane had entered the hall. Etienne strode toward her with purpose in his brisk steps. His mouth was bracketed with stern determination.

"Princess Ariane—"

He fairly announced her name, so booming and forceful was his voice.

"I've been looking everywhere for you," he said. "We're late for our ride. The stable hands have our horses saddled and ready."

Knowing that she hadn't accepted an invitation to

ride with the prince this morning, Ariane instantly realized that he must know what was going on and it was his intent to rescue her. From what folly, she hadn't a clue. But she thought it was sweet of him to come charging in like a white knight to sweep her away from the obvious unpleasantness she had been just about to encounter.

His smile was bright and in direct contrast with the staid faces of everyone else in the room, including the king and queen. His strong, tapered fingers slid over her forearm, and his touch sent electricity jolting over every inch of her skin.

"You'll need to change," he told her easily.

It was evident that he wanted her away from here. Away from the covert stares. Away from the friction that fairly crackled in the air.

For the span of a single heartbeat, Ariane hesitated. She really should stay to find out what the king had been about to say. But then she relented, turning to Etienne with a quick, flashing smile.

"I'm sorry if I kept you waiting," she told him.

She took his arm, and the two of them made their way down the length of the breakfast hall and out the door. Midway up the staircase, she asked, "Okay, what's happening?"

"Happening?"

She grinned. "Your tone tells me you're stalling. And you aren't doing it very well, either. You'll have to tell me eventually, you know. I can't apologize until I know what I've done wrong."

His hand covered hers, and his skin was warm against her own. She felt oddly protected.

Etienne's voice softened as he assured her, "You've done nothing to apologize for."

"Well, something was going on in there. Why else did you rush in to save me?"

By then they had reached the door to the guest suite.

Etienne looked uncomfortable, his handsome face taking on the same strain she'd seen in the expressions of the king and queen just moments before.

"What is it, Etienne?"

Just then a maid rounded the corner, a small stack of pristine white bath towels in hand.

"Let's go inside," he murmured the suggestion. "You're going to need a little privacy."

As Ariane pushed her way through the door, she said, "Francie's probably still here...."

But her eyes immediately swept the room and she could tell from the quiet that the two of them were alone.

"She and Harry are out and about again," Ariane told him. She turned to face him. "So what's this all about?"

For as long as she lived, she wouldn't look back on this moment without wanting to kick herself. She should have guessed what was coming. She should have known what had churned up the storm clouds.

"Ariane—"

He moved in closer, and she saw that his gray gaze contained flecks the color of slate. His hands slid up along her forearms and again she felt enveloped with a peculiar protectiveness.

"Your brother-in-law, Wilhelm Rodin, came to see my father late last night."

Fear spiked through Ariane like a bolt of lightning. "Lise? Is my sister okay? Is the baby all right?"

The panic she experienced regarding her pregnant sister's welfare had her trembling uncontrollably.

"He didn't say anything about Lise's health," Etienne told her. "I assume she's fine. There's no reason to think otherwise. From what I was told, she's on her way home to St. Michel."

"But why would she..." Confusion stole away the remainder of her query.

His beautiful mouth pursed into a firm, straight line. He sighed. "Ariane, there's no easy way to say this. Wilhelm came to my father requesting a decree of divorce from your sister."

Ariane gasped. "*What?* But why?"

Again, Etienne paused, and she got the distinct impression that he was steeling himself for the telling. What on earth could have happened between Lise and Wilhelm?

"He had some fantastic story," he said. "He told father that King Philippe had married when he was eighteen. To an American woman. And that he and this woman had a child together. He told us that there is a search being conducted. If the child is found, and if the child is male, then Philippe's first son will take over as king of St. Michel."

His pewter eyes looked pained, and Ariane had to let her gaze dip to the floor. She wasn't supposed to know this information. She had to act as if she were hearing it for the very first time. But, dear Lord in heaven, why would Wilhelm go to King Giraud with what was supposed to be a de Bergeron family secret? Why would the man divorce his pregnant wife? None of this made sense.

She knew the story couldn't stay hidden forever, but she never imagined it would be revealed like this.

"Wilhelm told my father that your father's first marriage to the American was never properly annulled." He leveled his gaze at her. "Ariane, if all this is true, then your father's marriage to your mother wasn't...legal. And that means, well, that you and your sisters are..."

He let the thought wither away as he was evidently unable to utter the word.

"Illegitimate," she finished for him. Her voice grated as she said, "My sisters and I are illegitimate."

Etienne's exhalation was so miserable sounding that Ariane got the impression that he had more to relay. And he did.

"Father has no choice but to grant Wilhelm his divorce," he said. "Wilhelm is claiming that his marriage to Lise took place under false pretenses. Of course, father will stall for a couple of days, however, Wilhelm was quite insistent." His tone quieted, intensified. "But you should also know that your brother-in-law went to the media. He sold the story to the highest bidder late last night. An article ran in one of those trashy gossip rags this morning. Other European papers are picking it up. I even heard a report on the BBC news this morning. The whole world is being alerted to what's taking place in the St. Michel royal house."

Ariane would never have guessed that this was how the story of her father's previous marriage would break. St. Michel was a small monarchy. There were several gossipy newspapers printed in her country, and the paparazzi were relentless in their pursuit of some tidbit of information on any member of the de Bergeron family. But she couldn't imagine that the people of the outside world would be the least bit interested in the St. Michel royals, or what took place behind their palace door.

She had imagined that she would be the one to tell Etienne about the plight that had befallen her and her sisters. And she'd planned to do it before leaving Rhineland. Well, that plan was worthless now.

Poor Lise! Her older sister must be devastated! She must be feeling lost and alone and scared to death. And Celeste wouldn't make her sister's homecoming an easy one, that was for sure. Wilhelm Rodin was a dirty, rotten scoundrel and that was all there was to it.

A dark cloud gathered as Ariane thought of her brother-in-law. The man had always been cold and calculating. Wilhelm had used the fact that he was a member of the royal house of Rhineland to convince King Philippe that a match between himself and Lise would unite their two countries. Ariane had felt uneasy about the marriage that their father had arranged for Lise. However, Lise had seemed content with it, so Ariane had kept her opinions to herself.

Pregnant and abandoned by her husband, Lise must be beside herself. At least Marie-Claire would be nearby. And Juliet and Georges. And sweet little Jacqueline would surely brighten Lise's days.

Even though Ariane worried about her older sister, she couldn't deny the utter joy that shot through her at knowing that the truth was finally out. She should be terribly distressed at the thought of losing her title, her social standing. But she wasn't. She felt…well, she felt liberated. No more official duties to perform. No more restraints on her behavior. She would very soon be able to start a whole new life for herself. One without official obligations or limits on her activities.

But first things first, she silently realized. She was in Rhineland on a mission. Just because the truth was out about her no longer being a princess didn't mean she stopped loving her country. She had a job to do. And she had every intention of doing it.

Etienne looked confused by her silence.

Finally, he softly asked, "You do realize what this means, Ariane? You do understand, don't you?"

Rather than jumping up and down in sheer delight as she wanted to do, she knew she had to once again clothe herself in her costume of shallowness and frivolity. And she had to do it quickly. For if she didn't, Etienne would certainly realize she'd been duping him all along. No princess in her right mind would be happy about having her title stripped from her.

"Oh, Etienne—" she collapsed against his chest, resting her head on his shoulder as she desperately tried to conjure some tears "—what in the world am I going to do? I've lost everything. *Everything*. I'm so humiliated."

She felt his body tense, and he moved in a manner that let her know he meant to lean away from her. Allowing him to look into her face now was out of the question. She had to summon up some real distress first.

Ariane clutched him to her, hugged him tight, all the while doing what she could to build up her anxiety.

"My friends will surely abandon me! I'll be shunned. I'll be a laughingstock."

With her body pressed so tightly against his, Etienne battled the desire chugging through him like a runaway locomotive. There was no stopping it. He should be ashamed of himself. Ariane was suffering a terrible torment. He should be comforting her…not imagining her naked in his arms.

But her breasts were firm. Her tummy, flat. Her hips, soft, curved. And she was so close. So very close.

Etienne closed his eyes. The insanity of passion pressed in on him just as tightly as she was, fogging his brain, stealing away his common sense.

He gulped in air. Fought the yearning that surged like liquid fire through his veins.

The defenselessness in her voice. The silkiness of her hair brushing against his neck like warm silk. The trembling of her body.

He wanted her. And, heaven help him, but he feared that submission was inevitable.

The hunger seething in him became greedy. It built in him like a frenzy until he thought he would go crazy with it. Finally, he did the only thing he could do. He surrendered.

Gently, he inched away from her. He tipped up her face until her anxious midnight eyes locked with his.

And then he covered her mouth with his own.

Chapter Five

Her lips were hot as brimstone and candy-sweet, just as he'd imagined they would be. He was vaguely aware of hearing a groan and instinctively knew it had originated deep in his own throat. He didn't even attempt to quell the sound of it, but let it rumble, low and sultry, a clear sign of all he was feeling.

His every thought had been consumed by this woman since her arrival in Rhineland. His sleep had been plagued by shadowy, sensuous dreams in which he'd touched and tasted, kissed and fondled. He'd become nearly obsessed with the hot and needy yearning she kindled in him.

She was playing some kind of game. He'd discovered that for certain the night they'd had dinner alone together. He'd pondered her behavior until he'd become scatty with bewilderment and frustrated beyond belief. But at this particular moment none of that mattered to him. *None of it.* All that filled his mind was his need. Right now, the need pulsing through him was a palpable thing. A living entity. To savor this moment was a necessity. To treat the here and now as if it might be his one and only chance to get this close to her.

The kiss was electric. Jolting. Shocking. Heat licked at every part of him like fiery flames. Engulfing him, consuming him. This was the kiss that filled every man's fantasy.

The thought made him balk…no, this kiss was *better* than any fantasy because it wasn't imagined or dreamed. *It was real.*

His tongue skittered along her luscious, velvety bottom lip. The taste of her ignited a fervor low in his gut. Blistering vines sprouted to life, a burning bush, curling, swirling inside him, stems and buds and leaves smoldering with heated desire. Growing. Spiraling. Until he was filled to the brim.

Nothing could extinguish the fire raging within him. He was helpless against it and knew that all he could do was let it blaze until it spent itself. Until it reduced itself to ashes.

Etienne lifted his hands, cradling her perfect face between his fingers. She felt so tiny. So vulnerable.

He kissed her mouth, her cheekbone, her eyelid, her temple. He pressed his lips against the silkiness of her hair. The faint scent of fresh rain filled his nostrils, fanning the wildfire of his passion to even greater heights. He wanted to get lost in her, to let the heat and the longing devour him, absorb him—*become him.*

His breath came in ragged gasps, and then he drew his head upright, dragging open his heavy eyelids in order to look down into her angelic face.

Her expression was like a douse of icy water against feverish skin.

There was desire in her indigo eyes, yes. Embers of it glowed white-hot, he could clearly see that. But there were other emotions, as well. Emotions that shook him to the core.

Confusion. Turmoil. And some other emotion that was inscrutable and impossible for him to decipher.

"Oh, Lord, Ariane—" he emitted a remorseful groan, his hands falling from her face to her shoulders "—what have I done? Forgive me. Please."

She tried to look away, but he lifted her chin, urging her gaze back to his.

"I've just delivered news that is sure to make you feel as if your whole world is about to crumble," he whispered. "And do I comfort you? Do I reassure you? No, instead I take full advantage of your weakness. I act like a—"

Disgust sliced through the rest of his thought, and he fell silent from the weight of the guilt that descended on him.

This morning, when his father had told him about Wilhelm and what was happening in the de Bergeron family, all Etienne could think about was how devastating this news was going to be for Ariane. Saving her from being hurt and disgraced had been his only thought as he'd rushed to reach her before anyone else could. But when he should have been strong for her…when he should have been a firm shoulder for her to lean on, all he had succeeded in doing was crumbling under his own plaguing desire for her.

He swallowed, and all he could bring himself to say was, "I'm sorry, Ariane. I truly am."

Silence, leaden and sluggish, turned the air hanging between them heavy with awkwardness.

Finally, he said, "I know what you must be feeling."

What he interpreted as a sad smile shadowed the corners of her mouth.

"No," she told him, her voice soft as a sigh. "I don't believe you do."

Self-reproach shot through him like a piercing arrow. Of course, he suddenly realized, he had no idea what she was feeling. How could he? Nothing like this had ever happened to him.

"You're right," he admitted. "All I can do is guess. And I would say that you have to be feeling overwhelmed. And afraid. Anxious about what the future will hold for you."

An intense yet unreadable expression crept across her beautiful features.

Something deep inside him compelled him to say, "This turn of events doesn't change who you are, you know. I mean that."

Now her deep blue gaze clouded, still indecipherable.

"Yes," he sadly admitted, "some people will turn their backs on you. There are those who will be unfeeling, even contemptuous of your predicament. You'll have to prepare yourself for that. But your friends...your *true* friends will stick by you, Ariane. You'll see."

He hoped she understood the silent implications behind his words. He wanted her to understand how he felt. Maybe he should just spell out his feelings. Maybe he should tell her in simple, no-nonsense language that she could count on him. But he didn't.

Whether the reason for that was the doubt he'd felt over the mask of shallowness she'd insisted on wearing since her arrival, or his own overwhelming confusion and uncertainty over how all this would or should affect his intentions toward her, he couldn't say.

His fingers firmed reassuringly on her shoulders. "Everything's going to be all right. That's the honest truth. Now, I want you to go put on your riding gear. I wasn't lying to you when I said the stable hands had saddled up some horses for us. As soon as Father told me the news about Wilhelm requesting attendance with him, I thought it would be best if I could save you from facing all those people at breakfast. I wanted to be the one to break the news to you, and my parents agreed that would be best. I called the stables to have the horses saddled and waiting, then I called your room, but you'd already left. I rushed to fetch you as quickly as I could."

She looked the epitome of innocence, and that ripped at the very heart of him. He wanted to gather her up in his arms. He wanted to protect her from this awfulness. But he dare not. He couldn't trust himself to do the right thing by her. Not with his passion still simmering just below the surface.

"Go on now," he told her, this time more firmly, and he let his hands fall to his sides. "Go get changed. All this will look less threatening after a nice, quiet ride."

He watched her turn and walk away from him, her bedroom door closing behind her.

Ariane couldn't have settled for a nice quiet ride even if her very life had depended on it. Wind whipped through her hair and her thigh muscles burned as she pressed them against the powerful body of the chestnut mare beneath her. Leaning forward over the animal's mane, she fairly stood in the stirrups as she tore across the Rhineland countryside. She could hear the hoofbeats of Etienne's horse just behind and to her left.

Overwhelmed. Afraid. Anxious.

Etienne had told her he imagined that these were the emotions she must be experiencing. And he was correct. However, he'd been completely wrong about the motive behind those feelings.

He'd been sure that her devastated expression had been due to the news he'd imparted. That the whole world now knew about her father's previous marriage—the marriage that made her and her sisters illegitimate and stole away her title of princess.

But that hadn't been what had rocked her world to its very foundations. Not at all!

She had been nearly knocked off her feet by that unexpected kiss he'd planted on her lips.

Her reaction to his touch had terrified her. Fearful that she wouldn't be able to suppress the passion that had exploded inside her like a blast from a flare gun, flickering and sparkling, rising heavenward at lightning speed.

She had been riddled with angst—was *still* riddled with it—over why he would show her such sweet and precious attention when he'd just discovered that she was illegitimate. That she was baseborn. That she had no royal title. That she no longer could offer him a thing: money, lands, social standing, reputation… nothing.

His behavior made no sense to her. Having had

weeks to anticipate his reaction to the news, she'd expected him to have nothing else to do with her once he found out she wasn't a legitimate de Bergeron...once he discovered that she could bring him no fortune, no lands. That she could bring his country no special economic favors. The loss of her title meant the loss of everything he—the crown prince of Rhineland—might find desirable in a marriage union with her.

So *why* had he kissed her? Why had he shown her such kindness when she'd predicted that he'd coolly yet politely disengage himself from her, inform her in no uncertain terms that there would no chance of their forming any kind of relationship?

The questions echoed mockingly through her brain as the horses' hooves pounded across the meadow.

There could be only one answer.

Pity.

Etienne felt sorry for her, for this plight she was facing. And he was just being nice. He'd consoled her. Assured her. Showered her with kind benevolence. That's all there had been to that kiss.

That conclusion stabbed through her heart like a double-edged knife, slicing her to the very soul. It was also what had her racing, hell-bent, over hill and dale.

She didn't want any man feeling sorry for her. She didn't want any man consoling her out of pity! Least of all Etienne!

A tiny ray of light shined through the frustrated darkness invading her mind. Maybe...just maybe, Etienne had kissed her because he was truly attracted to her. Maybe he didn't care that she could bring his kingdom no assets. Maybe he was simply a man who wanted a woman.

A man who wanted *her.*

He'd said the loss of her royal title didn't change who she was.

Come on, Ariane, a small, mean voice silently scolded. *You are not a stupid woman. You must realize that the disguise you've been wearing has made you look like a total idiot.*

There was no way on God's green earth that a man as intelligent and sophisticated as Etienne could feel attracted to a woman as addlepated as she'd led him to believe she was. The thought was utterly ridiculous.

So why *had* he kissed her? And why *had* he acted so intensely allured by her the night they'd dined together in his suite? If romance hadn't been the motivating factor behind his behavior—and it surely couldn't have been given the way she'd been forced to act—then what had been his intention?

Nothing good, that was for certain.

Pity could have spurred the kiss they had just shared, once again feeling sickened by the mere idea. But what about the other instances when they'd been alone and he'd become so tender and amorous? The times before he'd known about her illegitimacy?

The man was up to something. Of that there could be no doubt.

Had he known all along of the trouble brewing in St. Michel? Had his intention been to bombard her with romantic attention in order to get the scoop on what was happening in the de Bergeron Palace? Was he scouting for firsthand information on the search for the de Bergeron missing heir? Could it be possible that Etienne had been using her to get information just as she'd been using him?

The doubts and questions only further solidified her suspicion that Etienne himself might be behind the Rhineland plot to annex St. Michel.

But his kiss had just about melted the very soles of her shoes. His touch had stirred her desire in a way that she'd never before experienced. This man had some strange power over her. She hated to admit it, but it was true.

He touched her, and she became pliable as clay in his deft fingers. He kissed her, and she sizzled like the sun itself.

She'd have to fight the feelings this man brought out in her. She'd have to put her personal wants and desires aside. She might find her handsome prince alluring as the devil himself, but she must remember that he was most probably her worst enemy.

Etienne galloped up close, reached over and touched her forearm. Automatically, she reined in the mare.

"Whoa," she murmured as the animal slowed. "Whoa there."

He looked flushed, and more striking than ever before.

"I realize that you're upset," he told her with a grin. "But I'd rather you didn't run the legs off my best horses."

Ariane slid her hand down the mare's neck, patting it affectionately. "I'm sorry," she told him. "I just got caught up in my thoughts."

He caught hold of her reins. Their gazes clashed.

"I meant what I said before, Ariane. I totally understand your being upset by what's happening, but this won't matter to your true friends." His gray gaze intensified, as he added, "And I hope that's how you think of me. As a true friend."

He's lying. He's lying. He's lying.

Reality reverberated through her head like a chant. She had to keep telling herself the truth. No one else was here to do it. Yet at the same time she couldn't help admitting that all she really wanted to do was believe each and every one of his lies.

Aside from being outright rude, there had been no way for Ariane to escape the king and queen's invitation to the opera. Giraud and Laurette were proud of the famous European theater troupe they had lured to Rhineland for the season. The actors were talented enough, but the tragic opus had Ariane so bored that her eyes had begun to glaze over. She'd sent a silent prayer of gratitude heavenward when the lights of the theater had gone up, announcing intermission. The king, queen and their huge entourage of guests made their way to a private refreshment area where everyone feasted on a variety of champagne and other wines, caviar, cheeses and an assortment of imported exotic fruits.

"Are you enjoying the performance?" Queen Laurette asked her, flashing a bright and expectant smile.

"It's wonderful."

It wasn't a lie, Ariane decided as she watched the queen move on to converse with her other guests. The stage had been professionally transformed to replicate an eighteenth century Italian town square. The costumes were flawless in their historic design. The orchestral music and operatic songs were performed to utter perfection. It was just that Ariane found the opera—*all* opera, not just this one—tedious enough to bring her to tears.

She made small talk with several groups of people and sipped at a flute of sparkling pale champagne. Finally, she made her way toward the secluded alcove where Francie, Harry and Etienne stood talking.

The prince was dressed in his formal evening attire. The charcoal-gray jacket made his shoulders look broad and invited a woman's fingers to rove over them. Ariane was drawn to him like a moth to flame.

"He's going to leave her," she overheard Harry state. "That woman deserves to be abandoned to her fate."

Ariane knew Etienne's personal assistant was predicting the outcome of the opera's second act.

Francie gave his shoulder an intimate little push. "No woman deserves to be completely abandoned."

"This one does," Etienne agreed. "At best, she's a horrible mother. At worst, she's a murderer. Abandoning her is exactly what her husband should do. Get out while the getting is good, I say." Then he gave a small chuckle.

The sound of his laughter sent chills coursing down Ariane's spine. Why, oh, why did she find this man so alluring?

Nearly a week had passed since the news of her father's previous marriage had broken. In that time, Etienne had treated her as if she were made of delicate bone china. He'd insisted that everyone in the palace, servant and dignitary alike, treat her with the utmost respect, even angrily demanding that one government official take his leave from dinner when the man intimated that Ariane was no longer deserving of the royal treatment with which the Kroninbergs continued to present her.

Etienne had been kind and honorable toward her, and fiercely protective of her. And all the while, Ariane had been on her guard, watchful of some slipup on his part that would reveal to her the motives behind his wonderful behavior.

Oh, yes, he was very good at playing this game of cat and mouse. Much better than she, Ariane had to admit. All the pretense between them—he, acting the caring guardian and she, feigning the brainless wonder—had her nerves pulled taut to the breaking point every single day. She hoped to discover some fantastic piece of information about the Rhineland plot against St. Michel so that she could return to her country as soon as possible, for she didn't know just how long she could take the stress of this tremendous tension.

There was another reason she wanted to return to St. Michel. One that had nothing whatsoever to do with political intrigue.

Every time Etienne fought a battle for her—no matter how small, and no matter that she realized he must have ulterior motives—she felt her hold on her heart slipping a little more. She fought the tender emotions and the heated desires that raged inside her. She fought them hard. But it was a campaign she feared she was losing. If she didn't get away from this man soon, she was going to end up a casualty of war.

Francie saw her then, and waved for her to join them. "Ariane, tell us what you think. Does Cassandra deserve to be abandoned by her husband?"

Etienne turned, and there was something in his pewter gaze that made Ariane feel flushed with delicious heat from the roots of her hair to the tips of her toes.

"It does appear," Ariane said, "that Cassandra would never win a prize for Mother Of The Year. But raising six sons would be an overwhelming task for *any* woman, you have to agree. Her father died under mysterious circumstances, yes. However, no one but a crazy person commits murder without cause. And if you ask me, Cassandra isn't mad. If she killed her father, she must have had just cause. And if she's a murderer, think of the guilt she must be carrying around. Like baggage. Sometimes, a person's baggage can become so heavy that she—" Ariane shrugged one bare shoulder a fraction "—well, she just has to do something to lighten her load. Even if that something looks a little strange to everyone else." She grinned.

Francie and Harry laughed. Etienne just looked at her intently.

Finally, he murmured, "A very wise observation. I hadn't thought to delve into Cassandra's psyche to that extent."

Ariane's heart hammered. The manner in which his gray eyes pressed her, coupled with the realization that she'd stepped completely out of her role of inane behavior, had her feeling suddenly light-headed.

She chuckled gaily and decided to do what she could to cover her tracks. "Or our Cassandra could just be a spoiled little girl at heart. Maybe she killed off her father because he refused to give in to her every whim, and she intends to do away with the other men in her life because...well, because she's simply decided she hates the male of the species."

"Gruesome." Francie shuddered. "I hope she's

completely innocent. That's what I'm rooting for anyway."

"*You're* the innocent one, if you believe that," Harry said.

The four of them laughed, but Ariane didn't miss the curious light in Etienne's gaze as he studied her. Thankfully, the lights overhead flickered to signal that the second act was about to begin and everyone automatically gravitated back into the theater.

"Let's go find out what happens to Cassandra," Francie said to Harry, setting down her crystal flute on a nearby table. The couple left the alcove.

Ariane couldn't stop the smile that curled on her lips when she watched Francie stop long enough to share an intimate little tête-à-tête with Harry right there in the hallway, their heads together as they laughed.

"They certainly look happy," Ariane couldn't help commenting to Etienne.

"Harry seems to have fallen head over heels for Francie." One corner of his mouth quirked upward as he softly added, "And to think I was the one who set up their first date."

The remark had her looking at him quizzically.

A delighted twinkle lit his dove-gray gaze when he explained, "The night I invited you to have dinner with me in my rooms I asked Harry to waylay your lady."

Ariane actually gasped at the admission.

Etienne chuckled, lifting his hands palms up. "What can I say? I wanted to be alone with you."

Her blood raced at an alarming speed. Partly due to his flirtatious remark—she loved the idea that he'd wanted to be alone with her—and partly due to suspicion about why he'd admit to having Harry intercept Francie. The man was bent on keeping her off balance and in total confusion, it seemed.

Before she could think of an appropriate response, his expression took on a mischievous air. He looked around the nearly empty reception area. "Listen, would you mind too much if we missed finding out how the opera ends?"

"No. I wouldn't mind at all." Stung by self-consciousness over how quickly she answered, she purposefully slowed her speech, asking, "Why? Are you feeling ill? Do you need to go home?"

"I'm fine." He tossed a keen look her way. "It's you I'm worried about."

"Me?"

Etienne's grin was so sexy that Ariane felt her knees growing weak beneath her long flowing gown.

"Yes, you," he said. "Midway through the first act, you looked like you wanted to fidget and squirm right out of your seat."

Affronted, her spine straightened as she firmly pointed out, "Why...I've never fidgeted in my life."

His grin widened. "And as the performance continued, I was sure you might start snoring at any moment."

Shock had her mouth actually dropping open, her brow puckering. "I *do not* snore, Etienne Kroninberg!"

The teasing glint illuminating his gaze melted away her indignation.

"Hmmm." She rolled her eyes, suppressing the humor building up in her chest, tugging at her mouth. "Sounds to me as if you haven't been watching much of the opera, yourself. You've been spending your time watching me."

"Indeed," he murmured. Then he took her hand. "Come on, let's get out of here."

Ariane felt like a kid as the two of them rushed down the carpeted stairs and out the front doors to make their escape.

The restaurant they entered was gorgeously decorated in rich, dark woods. The wainscoted walls, the floors, the chairs, the tables, everything glowed with a polished patina that reflected the soft overhead lighting. Catering to the after-theater crowd, the establishment was nearly empty and would remain so until after the performance.

When the waitress showed them to a private table near the back, Etienne murmured something to the woman that Ariane couldn't quite make out. Ariane raised her brows at him as he held her chair and then slid into the one across from her and he explained, "I was ordering something special for us. A surprise. I hope you don't mind."

"Not at all," she told him easily, doing what she could to quell the thrill that shot through her to think that he'd want to surprise her with something special. She also couldn't deny that she was curious beyond measure.

Feeling the need for a diversion, she surrendered to the overwhelming urge to try to make him understand her feelings about tonight's entertainment.

"It's not that I don't like opera," she told him, looking guiltily down at where her hands were clasped on the tabletop. "I understand that the singers and actors work hard to perfect their craft. That it takes an army of people to accomplish all the tasks required to put on a performance of that magnitude. But, well, it's just that..." The rest of her thought faded and her shoulders sagged. She lifted her gaze to his. "Okay. I'll admit it. I don't like the opera."

Etienne rested his elbows on the table and his chin on his fists. "It is the most boring pastime ever invented, isn't it?"

Her eyes widened. She breathed, "You think so, too?"

He nodded. "A better word for how I feel about it might be tedious."

It was then that the waitress arrived with cups of steaming espresso for them both. And she placed a heavy porcelain custard cup in front of Ariane.

One look at the scorched sugar coating had her entire body reacting with glee. "Crème brûlée!"

Immediately, she checked her reaction. She sounded like a kid in a candy store. Even though she suffered a twinge of embarrassment over her childish squeal, she couldn't keep the delight out of her voice as she rationalized, "It's my favorite."

His gaze lit with merriment. "Well," he said on an exaggerated sigh, "if you have to miss the opera, you should miss it for something absolutely wonderful."

She'd already placed her napkin in her lap and picked up her spoon. But his words—the peculiarity in his tone—had her pausing. Her gaze found his, and when she realized to what he was referring, she felt her face flush hot with mortifying embarrassment.

"You know!" His expression told her she'd guessed correctly. "Oh, Etienne, I'm so sorry. You must think I'm positively horrible. You came to my homeland all those months ago and offered to take me out and I repaid the kindness by acting atrociously. I never meant for you to know that I left the opera house that night. I do hope you believe me." In an attempt to salvage at least some of her dignity, she pointed out, "I *did* get back before the end of the performance."

"That you did," he admitted with a chuckle. "And I appreciated the effort. Very much."

Of course, they were talking about the night when he'd traveled to St. Michel, before her father's death, to ask her to attend the opera with him. Feeling bored stiff with the performance, Ariane had talked Francie into stealing away for a bit. The two of them had left the theater for a quick snack. Ariane had ordered crème brûlée.

"But how did you know?" she asked, spooning up some custard and taking a taste. She closed her eyes to better enjoy the cool creaminess on her tongue.

"You had invited such a crowd to accompany us that night," he told her, "that I had completely lost sight of you at intermission. But Harry just happened to notice how you and Francie hung back after the break. He followed you when you left the theater. And like all good equerries, he reported everything to me later on."

Her groan was filled with self-loathing. "You must think I'm a terrible person. I *am* a terrible person." But then she groaned again, this time from sheer enjoyment as she swallowed. "Mmm. This is so good."

He laughed as he added a dollop of cream to his espresso and slowly stirred. Suddenly cognizant of her conduct, Ariane laughed, too. She put down the spoon in order that he might understand that she meant what she was about to say.

"I really am sorry, Etienne. It's just that, well..."

"It's just that crème brûlée is your favorite. And you dislike the opera." His tone was both matter-of-fact and filled with forgiveness.

She sighed. "Exactly."

They shared a warm chuckle, and then Ariane picked up her spoon and dug into her dessert with eager yet dainty relish.

He watched her, obvious pleasure curling his sexy mouth. Ariane couldn't help but recall the pleasure that mouth had given her not so very long ago. His kiss had been titillating. Arousing. Captivating.

Then she thought of Francie and Harry. Of the budding relationship the two of them were free to explore. Would she ever find that kind of happiness now that she'd lost her place in royal society? Who would want her now? Certainly not someone with a position as important as that of the man sitting across from her.

Etienne noticed that she'd stopped eating. "What's wrong? Is the—"

"No, no," she assured him. "The custard is delicious. Thank you very much for ordering it for me."

"What is it, Ariane?" he asked, refusing to be put off.

Never would she dare admit to him the reason for her sudden melancholy.

Instead, she softly replied, "I want to thank you for something else, too."

He looked at her with obvious interest.

"I want to thank you for the way you've treated me all week. You didn't have to, you know. Everyone would have said you were well within your rights to send me packing back to St. Michel."

He reached across the table and slid his hand overtop hers. Sparks seemed to zip and sizzle over her skin.

"Ariane, you've got to stop allowing this little problem to depress you so," he said.

"Little problem?" She wanted to laugh, but it stuck in her throat.

"I mean it," he continued firmly, the pad of his thumb roving back and forth across her flesh. "Look, for all you know the American woman your father married when he was eighteen could have met with some ill fate all those years ago. If she died before your parents married, then your title would be reinstated, wouldn't it? I know it's a long shot, but..."

Her spine straightened. "I never thought of that."

"And St. Michel is going to be just fine," he told her. "They'll find the missing heir. And if your half sibling is male, then they'll bring the gentleman back to reign as your father's successor."

She tilted her head just a fraction. "And if he's a she?"

Etienne lifted the fragile cup to his lips, took a sip, then replaced it on the saucer. "Then," he told her, "there's always the baby that Queen Celeste is carrying."

Ariane shook her head. "Yes, my stepmother does claim she's had tests that prove she's having a boy."

"See there—"

"But she's mean and conniving," she added, doing all she could to curb the bitterness she felt toward Celeste. "It wouldn't be beyond her to lie about a thing like that. And up to now she's refused to show anyone the actual test results. She won't even provide them to our prime minister."

"Well, she can't lie once the baby is born, now can she?"

Ariane didn't answer. There wasn't much that Celeste wasn't capable of.

"I think we need to change this gloomy subject," he said. And doing just that, he asked, "Since you've made it quite clear that you don't like the opera, what do you like to do for fun?"

"I enjoy riding."

His dark brows raised. "Every time you saddle up you nearly exhaust my horses."

"I like physical activities. Anything adventurous. Exciting." Her mind churned with possibilities. "Like, say, skydiving."

"I was afraid you were going to say something like that."

"It's not something I've ever tried," she admitted. "Yet."

He remained silent as he shook his head.

"I like hiking. Especially to places I've never seen before."

"Now there's something more my speed."

Ariane finished the last bite of her custard and dabbed the white linen napkin to her lips. "It's hard to have fun, though, when the security people are dogging your every move. I know it's their job to protect me, but it would be great to escape them. Just for a bit."

It had been an offhand remark. One that she and her sisters had repeated to one another many times over: their wish to be free of the watching eyes of security personnel, and the ever-present reporters who forever seemed to be looking for the scoop of the century. With so many people following and harassing a body, it was nearly impossible to go anywhere or do anything without everyone and their mother knowing about it.

However, her complaint prompted something in Etienne. It was clear that his mind was churning, his thoughts spinning. Finally, he leaned toward her, his cool gray eyes glinting with mischief, and said, "I'm up for a little adventure and excitement." One dark brow lifted, inquiringly. "Are you?"

Chapter Six

He'd learned something tonight, Etienne decided as he shrugged out of his formal jacket and tossed it onto the bed. Ariane wasn't like any other woman he'd ever met.

Yes, he'd suspected it. All those months ago when he'd gone to St. Michel, and even more so since her visit to his own homeland. The thought had even flitted in and out of those hot, shadowy, increasingly erotic dreams that featured her every time he fell asleep. However, the fact that she was amazingly and wonderfully different from any other female he'd encountered had been solidified in his mind when he'd witnessed the gleeful light in her gorgeous deep blue gaze when he'd suggested that the two of them slip away from the opera tonight. Like a power switch that had been suddenly thrown, an impish energy seemed to palpitate from her.

The absolute wicked naughtiness that had curled the corners of her sexy mouth as they had left the theater, hand in hand, had had Etienne silently vowing that, if Ariane enjoyed breaking the rules as much as she seemed to, then he was willing to become a fun-loving rebel right along with her. She was like a breath of fresh air. And being with her filled him with a robust exhilaration.

He'd so enjoyed her display of shock in the restaurant when he'd revealed he'd been privy all along to her behavior when he'd taken her on that fiasco of a first date. He believed her apology had been sincere. His heart had been touched by her earnest appeal. She really hadn't meant to hurt or embarrass him that night. He realized it. Her exuberance for life—and her love of crème brûlée—had made it impossible for her to sit through the tragic opera he'd taken her to see.

A man couldn't hold a grudge over something like that, now could he?

Etienne chuckled as he changed out of his suit and into jeans, a sweater and a pair of sturdy hiking boots. Then he hurriedly tossed a change of clothes, a comb and his toothbrush into a knapsack. He wasn't certain where he was going to take her or exactly when they'd return, so he decided to go prepared. He'd told her to do the same.

Feeling like an errant youngster flushed with the excitement of running away from home, he slung the pack over his shoulder, shut the door of his suite and went to fetch Ariane.

His knuckles had barely touched her door when she opened it to him.

"I'm ready."

Her midnight eyes danced with an exhilaration that was utterly beguiling and it was all he could do not to tell her she looked ravishing. However, he knew he'd best focus on his goal of getting them out of the palace unnoticed by the security personnel or else he just might give in to the desire that sat smoldering in his belly like glowing embers.

In that instant, Etienne paused, wondering exactly what he was doing. It had been his intention in pursuing Ariane to land himself a wife who was a princess. A woman of royal blood. A noblewoman who could rule Rhineland by his side when he became king. However, although Ariane had been born and raised as an aristocrat, she'd lost her royal standing. He should be putting distance between them, not running off on an adventure with her.

Ariane picked up her canvas knapsack, but after taking one look at his face, she asked, "You okay?"

He smiled. "Fine," he said. "I'm just fine. Let's go." Taking her hand in his, he tugged her out into the hallway.

They laughed like kids and talked about every topic under the sun on the drive to Rhineland's largest national park. He told her of some of his and Harry's exploits when they'd attended Eton together. And she recounted some of her own teenage misadventures with her sisters. She told him about attending school in Switzerland and how she'd missed her family.

Etienne knew from a college psychology course that middle children were usually quiet, self-conscious overachievers who strived for attention that was typically showered on either the older or younger siblings. However, it didn't seem that Ariane fit that mold at all. She was self-confident, outgoing and clearly unafraid of taking risks. Etienne discovered that those qualities appealed to him. Very much.

"Right after my stepmother, Helene, died," she

said, seemingly eager to recount another escapade from her youth, "my sisters and I slipped down into the wine cellar with my stepbrother, Georges, and my stepsister, Juliet. All of us got a little tipsy before we were discovered."

Her chuckle chimed like soft bells in the darkness of the car. Then he heard her sigh.

"Georges was eighteen," Ariane continued. "He was old enough to know better. So was my oldest sister, Lise." Again she laughed and admitted, "So was I, actually. But all of us had been grief-stricken for days and days. The whole household was morbidly silent. Father had been desolate over Helene's death. And the loss of another stillborn son."

Etienne felt her eyes on him.

Her voice softened as she admitted, "I guess all of us kids were just looking for some way to break out of our sadness. We were giggling like monkeys when the housekeeper found us."

After a moment, Etienne asked, "How did your father feel about the method you used to...er, overcome your sorrow?"

White teeth flashed in the shadows when she smiled. "Oh, we'd only opened two bottles, so we hadn't imbibed all that much." Then she whistled. "But Father's neck veins began to protrude when he learned we'd opened two of the rarest wines in his collection."

"Angry, was he?"

She was quiet for a moment, and he sensed rather than saw her shake her head. It was then that he realized she was recalling what must be a vivid memory from her past.

"Yes, but in the end he forgave us all. We had a secret weapon, you see."

Etienne was silent as he waited for her to elaborate.

"We sent Marie-Claire to plead our case for us. She was Father's favorite." Again, she paused. "It wasn't the first time, or the last, that she got us out of trouble. She had Father wrapped around her little finger."

Being an only child of parents who enjoyed a stable and loving relationship, he couldn't imagine what it must have been like to grow up in a family that consisted of siblings, stepsiblings, half siblings, stepmothers and nannies.

"Did that bother you?" he couldn't help but ask. "Your father having an obvious favorite, I mean?"

She exhaled softly. "I'd love to be able to say it didn't bother me in the least. But I believe there isn't a little girl alive who doesn't want to be the apple of her father's eye."

Ariane's soulful tone did something odd to him, and he made a silent vow there and then that if he were to have children he'd never give one child more esteem than another. He'd love each and every one of his children just as exuberantly as the next.

"The fact that Marie-Claire was Father's pet didn't affect my relationship with my sister," she said. "Luckily, I realized early on that it wasn't her fault. And I loved her dearly for getting me out of trouble when she could." She grew still suddenly. "But I did learn something from it."

Etienne pulled the car into the empty parking lot and cut the engine. He sat in the quiet darkness, hoping against hope that she wouldn't make him ask the question that rolled around in his mind.

Thankfully, she put his curiosity to rest.

"I learned that love shouldn't be treated like a pie. The pieces shouldn't get smaller with each portion that's served. And no one deserves a bigger slice than anyone else."

Softly, he said, "I agree." He marveled that their thoughts were so much in tune.

There was a forlornness in her tone that made him believe that there had been times during Ariane's childhood when she'd felt lost—and very hurt—by her father's preferential treatment of her younger sister. Oh, Ariane was attempting to handle the matter maturely, and Etienne found that quite an engaging attribute, but it was clear to him that she was bothered by it, nonetheless.

He'd have loved to pull her to him, to hug away all the bad feelings that might be festering inside her, to convince her somehow, some way that she was just as lovable as Marie-Claire. But all he did in the end was to gently reiterate, "No one deserves a bigger slice of love then anyone else."

They were quiet for some time, and the air seemed to crackle and rumble with a stormy awareness. However, before things had a chance to become uncomfortably awkward, Ariane focused her gaze out the windshield at the forest ahead.

"So, where are we?" she asked.

"Byron Park. Named for my great-great-great-great-grandfather." He looked at the dark path and wondered now if bringing her here had been the wisest choice. "I haven't been here in years, but I camped here as a boy. I had a great time on that mountain, and I remember this place was simply awesome at night." He eyed her thoughtfully. "But I'm having second thoughts about this adventure. Maybe we should wait until daylight—"

"Are you kidding?" She opened the door and exited the car as she spoke. "The moon is full. Just like a huge flashlight." When he didn't get out immediately, she leaned over and peered at him. "I love hiking. And I've never done it at night. This will be fun. Come on!"

He had no recourse but to get out of the car, too. Hesitation had him saying, "But what about—"

"No buts," she cut in. "We'll be perfectly safe. This is Europe, remember. The most dangerous animal we're likely to meet is a hungry chipmunk."

He laughed. "The danger I was thinking of is all those tree roots out there waiting to trip us up. One of us is bound to break an arm or leg."

Waving off his dire prediction, she grabbed her backpack from the rear seat, shrugged into it and set off toward the path. Etienne reached for his pack and followed her.

"Wait for me!" he called.

Ariane had been right, he soon realized. The moon illuminated the path in most places, but he grew to look forward to the areas that were thickly wooded and deep in shadow for those were the times when he took her hand. Solely for safety reasons, of course.

"What are you chuckling at?" she asked, when he slid his palm against hers on a dark part of the trail.

"Oh, nothing." A conversation was what he needed now. His mind whipped through possible topics. Finally, he said, "You've spoken of your father, your stepmother, your siblings. But you haven't said anything about your mother. What kind of person was she?"

For a moment, all he heard was the rustle of the leaves overhead.

Then she said, "There's not a whole lot to tell. I don't remember much about her. You see, my parents divorced when I was three. Over the course of her marriage to my father, my mother gave birth to three girls. The story goes that she wasn't interested in having any more children. My father was desperate for a male heir, so they decided it was time for their relationship to come to an end. He says he really didn't have a choice."

She tugged her hand from his, reaching up to her shoulder to grip the harness of her knapsack. Her whole body seemed to tighten, alerting Etienne that the end of the story wasn't going to be pleasant for Ariane.

"My mother was what you might call a jet-setter, and apparently eight years of marriage were more than enough for her," she said, seeming to pay close attention to where she planted her feet on the dirt path. "She couldn't wait to get out of St. Michel." She quietly added, "Away from her family." Ariane sighed deeply, almost as if steeling herself. "She spent her time skiing in Aspen, gambling in Monte Carlo, sailing the Riviera, soaking up the sun in Fiji. She never missed the America's Cup finals, or the running of the bulls in Pamplona, or the Wimbledon tournaments, or a dozen other events in a dozen other countries. Her lifestyle didn't leave her much time to be a mother to her children. But that didn't seem to bother her. Lise, Marie-Claire and I remained in our father's custody after our mother left. We were raised by nannies for the most part. We did see our mother occasionally. A couple of times a year. But..."

Whatever else she was going to say vanished like a thin night mist and Etienne was sorry he'd broached the subject in the first place.

Ariane continued, "She died many years ago. In a scuba diving accident somewhere near the Great Barrier Reef."

So essentially Ariane had grown up without a mother...and often feeling as if she were playing second fiddle to her youngest sister for her father's affections. She must have experienced many lonely and confusing times as a child. Etienne's heart broke for her. Yet he marveled that the experiences of her youth didn't seem to have had any adverse effect on her personality.

The instinct to protect her welled up in him something fierce. In answer, he reached out, and sliding his palm up her forearm, he gently pried her fingers loose from the strap of her backpack and held her hand firmly in his even though the pathway ahead was brightly lit by the fat full moon that hung in the silky night sky.

The smile she offered was small, and sad, her face luminous in the reflected light, and he felt as if his heart were some kind of powerful engine *thub-thubbing* in his chest.

"My father's second wife, Helene—"

Suddenly Ariane stopped speaking, then tilted her head as if an idea just occurred to her.

"—I guess Helene was Father's third wife. I'm having trouble remembering that." She shook her head. "Anyway," she went on, "Helene tried to be a good stepmother to me and my sisters. Of all of Father's wives, Helene is the one I hold closest to my heart. She was the widow of an old friend of Father's,

d after she and Father married, she was very pre-
cupied with trying to give my father the baby boy
so needed. It was almost as if Helene and my fa-
er had some sort of arrangement, or agreement. She
as looking for a father for her children, Georges and
liet, and father wanted an heir. ''

''A marriage of convenience,'' Etienne murmured.

Ariane nodded.

''Those kinds of relationships are quite routine in
r world, you know,'' he quietly pointed out.

If the truth were known, he'd actually thought of
fering Ariane the same sort of arrangement when
'd first traveled to St. Michel all those months ago.
ve himself a lot of trouble by cutting through all
e formalities and offering the woman a deal. A
ion between their royal families that would afford
th their countries some benefits. Ariane's father,
ng Philippe, had hinted that he would be open to
ch an offer.

However, after having met Ariane, after having ex-
rienced firsthand her feisty nature, he simply hadn't
en able to bring himself to make the proposition.
e'd liked her. From the first. And although putting
rward a bargain was the route he probably should
ve taken, he hadn't wanted to stilt any possible fu-
re he might have with Ariane with awkward official
fers that would surely lead to something less than
e real thing. And his gut had told him Ariane wasn't
e type of woman who would react favorably to an
fer of marriage that was based on political or eco-
mic reasons.

After that first meeting, he'd planned to visit St.
ichel again just as soon as Ariane had had time to
ieve for her father and his mother had had time to

regain her health. But then Ariane had arrived i
Rhineland—and he'd been ecstatic about the idea tha
she might be responding to his interest in her. Unt
her odd behavior had him guessing there were ulteric
motives behind her visit.

"Well, even if Father and Helene married becaus
of some kind of bargain they made," Ariane said, "
still loved the woman. It was she who brought Jacque
line into my life."

"Your youngest sister?"

Ariane nodded. "My half sister, really. She's lik
a ray of sunshine in that house, Etienne. You'll hav
to meet her. She's just a wonderful little girl. Curiou
and bold. Full of spirit."

He grinned. "A little like you, huh?"

Her mouth pulled back warmly. "I don't kno
about that. I just know that she and I share a stron
bond. Jacqueline is the reason I've stayed at the pal
ace. I could have moved out. Would have preferre
to, actually, since Father's death. There are severa
summer cottages and town houses for the choosing
but I just couldn't leave my baby sister to fend fc
herself against Celeste. Jacqueline is only twelve
She's needed a protector since Father passed away."

Again, she grew still, vulnerability fairly pulsin
from her.

"I've worried about her since I've been gone. I'v
talked to her several times on the phone. Grandmam
and Marie-Claire both promised to look after her."

She glanced up at the stars as if offering up a siler
prayer.

"I hope she's okay. I hope Celeste hasn't crushe
her spirit." Ariane sighed glumly.

Etienne gave her hand a reassuring squeeze. "I'

re she's doing just fine. Come on, now,'' he chided, e poignancy expressed in her deeply furrowed brow awing at the very heart of him. ''We're here to have n, remember?''

''You're right.'' Her chin tipped up suddenly and e seemed to shake off the bad thoughts. Suddenly, e paused, her head tilting a fraction to one side. Listen. What's that?'' Before he could answer, her hole face lit up like a hundred-watt bulb. ''A wa- rfall! I can hear it. Come on!''

Without releasing his hand, she broke into a jog, gging him along with her.

The falls was what he'd brought her here to see. s a boy, the sight of the rushing water had never ft his mind. He'd wanted to share this with her.

''Oh, Etienne,'' she breathed almost reverently, he water looks just like liquid silver. It's just beau- ul.''

The cascading water was beautiful yes, but not arly as beautiful as her face. Her dark eyes shined, r full, perfect lips were partially open. The awe she obviously felt was clearly articulated on her face. e realized at that moment that he'd like to experi- ce every aspect of life with her…through her eyes. e loved the way she become so caught up in the oment.

''A Rhineland poet once described the falls as umbling moonlight,''' he told her.

''The description fits perfectly.''

''The river is spring fed. The water bubbles up om deep inside the mountain. It's crystal clear and rfectly safe to drink.''

She blinked, then turned her gaze on his. Her eyes ittered with renewed excitement. ''The pool is just

lovely. I'm sure the water's freezing now. But if i
were summer, I'd love to have a swim.''

He remained silent, but made a mental note of he
remark. If it was at all possible, he'd bring her bac
once summer arrived.

''Can we climb to the top?'' she asked.

''Of course.'' He answered quickly, catching th
fever of her delight. He'd have given her the stars i
she'd asked for them. Now, he only hoped he had th
stamina to back up his promise and make the stee
climb. ''Wait for me,'' he found himself callin
again, and he trotted after her.

Later, they sat on the mossy ground, completel
spent from the strenuous ascent. He studied her per
fect profile.

There were other ways in which he'd rather tir
himself out, he couldn't help but think. Ravishing he
luscious lips with his own would be high on his list
As would peeling the clothing off her delectable bod
and touching her, loving her, all over.

''What are you thinking about?'' she asked. Sh
lifted the bottle of water to her mouth and took
swallow.

Etienne actually felt his face go ruddy and hot, an
he was relieved that her attention was focused on th
swift current that carried the spring water bubblin
over rocks and boulders on its way to the falls rathe
than on him. He took a deep breath and did what h
could to banish the erotic images from his mind.

But doing so, he promptly discovered, proved
difficult task.

''Not a thing,'' he said at last. ''I'm just trying t
recover. It isn't easy keeping up with the likes o
you.''

She grinned. "You're earning lots of points by the
ıere fact that you're trying." Her smile faded then,
ıd her tone grew whisper soft as she added, "But
r the life of me, I can't understand why you
ould."

The reasons were mounting, he thought to himself.
et at the same time, he had to admit that the thought
asn't ever too far away that reminded him there
ere serious reasons why he shouldn't. Luckily,
ough, he didn't have to respond because she chose
at instant to stifle a yawn.

"It's late," he told her. "And we're both tired. We
ould get back to the car."

"I'm not just tired. I'm exhausted." She stretched
ıt, laid her head on his lap. "Can we just rest for a
it first?"

"Sure."

Etienne reclined against the massive tree at his
ack and gazed down at Ariane. Her chest rose and
ll in an easy, rhythmic motion. Her honey-blond
air glowed golden in the bright moonlight, her dark
shes cast fan-shaped shadows high on her milky
ıeekbones.

Desire quickened inside him.

He'd learned many things about Ariane tonight.
he hadn't had the best of childhoods. Over the years
r family had consisted of a conglomeration of step-
others, siblings and stepsiblings. Yet she'd grown
ıto a confident, vivacious woman. She cared deeply
out her sisters and her brother. She couldn't sit
rough an opera without becoming bored to tears,
ıd she'd risk an international incident in order to
ıjoy a crème brûlée. He grinned. He'd also learned
at she looked just as good in jeans and hiking boots

as she did in silk and high heels. The yearning he felt for her swirled low and hot, warming him to the marrow.

Etienne had discovered some things about himself, too. First and foremost, he liked Ariane. No, he more than liked her. And he sure as hell desired her.

In fact, he'd realized that he was falling hopelessly in love with the woman.

Sighing, he closed his eyes and tried to relax. But the notions eddying in his head made that next to impossible.

All of these realizations posed a huge problem for him.

He'd gone out seeking a wife. A princess. His parents fully expected him to fulfill that goal.

Yet here he was at the top of Byron Mountain after having run away in the night with a woman who had no title, no fortune, no lands…not even a social standing to offer him and his country.

Had he totally lost his mind?

Or just his heart.

Chapter Seven

Ariane opened her eyes, inhaling a deep, sleepy reath. The scent of Etienne wrapped her in a snuggly lanket and had her releasing a contented sigh. The ound of his heartbeat against her ear made her lips ull back in a drowsy smile. His chest made a won-erful pillow. She should feel self-conscious by the itimate manner in which her palm was splayed gainst his flat abdomen, the way her body was ressed up close to his, but her brain was much too uzzy to give the notion more than a fleeting thought. ll she wanted to do was lower her eyelids and slip ack into her restful slumber.

A moment or two later wakefulness nudged at her. he extricated herself from Etienne's cozy embrace, arveling at how they had become so entangled on the ossy ground during the night. She'd only meant to st her eyes and her tired body for a few moments, but e saw that the sky was turning pink with a new day.

Ariane realized that she'd never spent the night under the stars before. She'd never slept in a man's arms before, either.

She sat up, stretching the kinks out of her muscles. She didn't think she'd ever roused with such a feeling of peacefulness. Was the feeling brought on by her having slept outdoors? Or because for hours and hours she'd been cuddled in Etienne's arms? It wouldn't take a rocket scientist to figure this out, she silently surmised.

Reality slowly seeped through her sleep-fogged brain, churning up her thoughts and her emotions, and dragging her into the fully conscious world.

As she stared down at the gorgeous prince in slumber, she couldn't decide if this outing made her delirious with happiness or crestfallen with utter misery. Elated that Etienne would abscond from his royal duties, she realized that he possessed a bit of an adventurous spirit that closely matched her own. She'd enjoyed the trek up to Byron Falls. She'd been enchanted by the stories of Etienne's past. She'd taken great pleasure in telling him about her own. Their time together seemed to sparkle like the stars in the predawn sky. All in all, the evening had been soul-stirring.

So had Etienne.

However, the wretched facts remained: he was the crown prince of Rhineland, and even though he could play at courting all the women he wanted, he could never settle down with any female who didn't have an impeccable name and reputation.

She didn't fit either category. She'd known that even before arriving in his country. And now he knew it, too.

Ariane watched him sleep, his features relaxed, the

rustic shadow of whiskers on his jaw making him devastatingly desirable. It was all she could do not to reach out and run her hand over his flat stomach. She wondered what it would be like to slip her fingers underneath his sweater and tangle them in the springy hairs of his chest peeking out from the neckline.

After getting to know him, she found it difficult to envision him trying to do something as unscrupulous as usurping a neighboring country. He had a strong character, yes. He would make a great king someday. But there was a difference between a man who was powerful and one who was heartlessly ruthless.

The cool morning breeze had her unwittingly rubbing her hands up and down her forearms. Snatching up her pack, she walked to the creek and then along the gurgling water until she found a spot private enough to refresh herself. She splashed cold, clear spring water over her face, then pulled her toothbrush out of her pack and cleaned her teeth.

The sun was just coming up over the horizon, turning the sky a glorious crystal blue, when she returned to the spot where they had slept together and found Etienne and his backpack gone. Before she had time to feel even a moment of concern, however, he broke through the trees and smiled at her.

The manner in which her heart lurched at the mere sight of him hinted that her feelings for this man were more serious than they should be. That thought was worrisome.

"Good morning," he said. "I was just cleaning up a bit...and answering the call of nature."

Ariane grimaced. "Nature's calling me, too, but..." She glanced around, disliking the idea rolling around in her head.

He chuckled. ''Not to worry. There's a public restroom just twenty yards or so down that path. That's where I've just come from.'' He pointed in the direction from which he'd just come.

Her shoulders sagged with gratitude. ''Thanks.'' And she toddled off to use the facilities.

When she returned, he said, ''I hadn't expected to spend the night outside. How'd you sleep?''

''Fine, but I am feeling a little stiff,'' she admitted.

''Were you cold in the night?''

Ariane simply shook her head in answer, remembering how she'd had to untangle herself from him. He had kept her toasty warm all night long, but she didn't feel comfortable making that confession.

''D-did you sleep well?'' she asked, unable to meet his gaze.

''A soft mattress would have been nice.'' He looked at the horizon, stretching his broad back and shoulders this way and that. ''But the walk down to the car will surely loosen us both up, don't you think?''

She nodded, realizing that he, too, sensed the awkward air that had crept over them. It was clear that he was doing all he could to avoid mentioning the fact that they had slept together. Granted, they hadn't shared a single sensuous touch or one whispered word of want, but there was still something amazingly intimate in the notion that they had spent the night in each other's arms.

''I'm starved,'' she blurted, feeling the sudden need to fill the silence that surrounded them.

''Then our first order of business is finding some breakfast.''

Worry wrinkled the bridge of her nose. ''It's a long drive back. Maybe we should return to the palace. If you don't show up for breakfast everyone will be up in arms.''

''Nonsense,'' he said, waving off her concern. Conspiratorially, he whispered, ''I don't know if you've noticed, but I'm all grown-up. It'll be okay if we spend the day together.''

She cast him a dubious glance. ''Being grown-up is one thing, but worrying your parents by disappearing without a word is quite another.''

''Okay, okay,'' he appeased. ''I'll call home as soon as we can find a phone. Will that make you happy?''

The smile with which she graced him was clear evidence that it did.

He took her hand in his like it was the most natural thing in the world, and the unwieldy moments seemed to scatter like the darkness of night chased away by daybreak.

It would be lovely to forget, just for a little while, that he was a prince and she was a woman who had lost her title—and with it every chance she might have had with a man like Etienne.

Yes, forgetting reality would be lovely, indeed.

The tiny roadside café catered to tourists, a prime source of Rhineland's revenue, and the place was buzzing with travelers even at this early hour. However, because Etienne and Ariane were dressed as they were in jeans, jackets and heavy hiking boots, and the fact that they both looked a little rumpled from their night spent at Byron Falls, they were able to sit at a table right next to the window and enjoy their coffee while gazing out at the beautiful view of the rolling hills without being recognized.

"So," Ariane said to him, "your parents were okay with us slipping off?"

He nodded. "Everything is fine. Father was a tad miffed that we slipped away from the opera last night. But he was happy that I called. I want to thank you for encouraging me to get in touch with him. That was very thoughtful of you."

She gazed at him over the rim of her cup, some unreadable emotion clouding her beautiful eyes.

"They really don't mind your spending the day with me?"

"Absolutely not," he said. "Father told me to show you a good time. He knows you've been under a great deal of stress lately."

The sigh she expelled had him asking, "What is it, Ariane? Something's bothering you. Tell me what's on your mind."

"It's nothing."

But her tone was whisper soft and she'd averted her gaze out the window. When she looked at him next, a smile had returned to her lips.

"This is nice," she said.

He knew without asking that she meant the picturesque town he'd brought her to, the charming café, being out in public unnoticed, the freedom from personnel whose sole goal was to protect and defend, being away from the prying eyes of the press.

"It *is* nice," he agreed. "In fact, I have to admit to feeling a bit envious of your new beginning."

A confused frown bit into her delicate brow. "My new beginning?"

"Your life is going to burst forth with color and freshness and fragrance—" he grinned "—like spring bulbs erupting from the earth. Just think, no protocol to follow, no etiquette to worry about, no official duties to perform.'' Although he could actually hear the covetousness in his tone, he didn't feel the least bit self-conscious when he added, ''No rules to follow. No one to answer to.''

She just looked at him.

''Oh, what I wouldn't give to be in your shoes.''

Wasn't it funny? he thought. He'd planned this spur-of-the-moment jaunt of theirs as a means of getting Ariane to open up to him. Being the high-spirited woman he had come to know her to be, he realized that she'd never be able to turn down an opportunity to experience a little adventure, and she'd agreed to run away with him without a moment's hesitation. However, rather than coercing her to reveal her deepest thoughts and feelings to him, here he was exposing his own wishes and desires.

Finally, she tilted her head and grinned at him, and he thought the expression was sexy as the dickens.

''Come on now.'' There was chastisement in her tone. ''No rules and no one to answer to is a great concept, but you can't sit there and tell me that you're envious of my illegitimacy.'' She moistened her lips, and when next she spoke, her voice grew serious. ''I may have gained some freedom, Etienne, but my father's actions—and the fact that my grandparents kept all of it a secret—have cost me everything.''

Ariane was a strong woman, Etienne knew. But whenever she displayed any sense of vulnerability, all he wanted to do was scoop her up into his arms and protect her from the world.

He slid his hand overtop hers. Her skin felt hot against his. And silky smooth. Little zips of current seemed to stick him like tiny needles.

"I've said this before—" he leveled his gaze on her so she'd realize his utter sincerity "—the news regarding the circumstances of your birth doesn't change who you are inside."

She swallowed, her midnight gaze growing haunted. Softly she said, "But it sure does change a lot. For me and my sisters. Look at what's happening to Lise. Wilhelm has left her high and dry, Etienne. And she's pregnant. I talked with Marie-Claire yesterday morning and she told me that our wonderful stepmother has refused to allow Lise to move back into the palace."

"She can't do that."

"Oh, can't she? You don't know Celeste." Ariane could only shake her head. "I'm sure the woman isn't interested in having any more competition around her. That's how she always saw us, you know, as competition. For everything. My father's affections. The royal coffers. Even the public's fondness, interest and attention." The sound she made was filled with disgust. "Just everything."

Myriad emotions seemed to ooze from her in waves, yet all he could do was sit there and listen.

"There is so much controversy surrounding the baby Celeste is carrying," she continued. "There are even doubts being expressed by some over who fathered this child."

Lord above, Etienne thought silently. He'd known St. Michel's royal house was in an uproar, but he hadn't guessed the family had been experiencing this kind of turmoil.

"Do you think your stepmother is capable of doing something like that?"

"Is she capable? Yes."

Ariane's voice sounded small, and he was hit yet again with the urge to protect her from harm, from all negative emotion.

"But I sure hope she didn't," Ariane added. "She couldn't get away with a thing like that. Not with the DNA testing that's available today. And government officials will eventually require it. I know the prime minister won't let Celeste get out of it, no matter how she fights it."

"I would think proving the legitimacy of her child would have her running to take the tests."

She nodded. "Now you can better understand why there's so much controversy swirling around her pregnancy."

The waitress arrived with their platters of food, and Etienne smiled as he watched Ariane pick up her fork and dig in with enthusiasm. For some reason, he thoroughly enjoyed the idea that she loved to eat a good, healthy meal. He'd never been attracted to wafer-thin women, and although she could never be described as overweight, her body was luscious and curvy. Like a warm, ripe peach just waiting to be plucked. And savored.

He allowed himself a moment to close his eyes and imagine biting into a juicy piece of fruit, dream of the heady taste as syrup dribbled down his chin unchecked. Desire quickened inside him and his eyelids flew open, his gaze zeroing in on Ariane's full, rounded breasts, his salivary glands working overtime. He forced his eyes to her pink lips. He'd kissed her mouth. Had sampled the sweetness of her. Oh, how he'd love to relish the whole of her.

Etienne was besieged with a strange shakiness. This woman did things to him that no other had.

"Is something wrong?"

"No," he lied. Picking up his fork and knife, he focused his attention on his plate. He inhaled a deep breath in a vain attempt to quell the throbbing of his blood through his veins. Once again, he was amazed by how she stirred his libido. But his desire for her wasn't purely lust alone. He wanted to get inside her head, to know what she thought about life. He wanted to discover what made her laugh, what made her sad, what made her angry, what made her proud. He wanted to know all there was to know about her.

In an effort to make some forward strides in this quest, he asked, "How do you feel about the law your government has that states only male heirs can sit on the throne?"

Her eyes grew hooded. Was that distrust he saw clouding her features? But before he could decide, her gaze cleared somewhat. As she chewed, her shoulders lifted in a small shrug. Finally, she swallowed. "Of course, it's an archaic law. One that's demeaning to all women, not just the females of the de Bergeron royal family. If I could do something to change it, I would." Again she shrugged. "But I can't."

Although she was presenting a face of casual indifference to something she could do nothing about, Etienne sensed that she was deeply hurt by her government's inability to acknowledge that women were capable of acting as sovereign leader.

He found it impossible to still his tongue on the matter. "I think someone ought to change the idiotic law. Can't the officials of your country see that it could have a devastating effect on St. Michel?"

Etienne pressed his lips together. He hadn't meant to bring up her country's governmental problems.

During the weeks she'd been in Rhineland, he'd had his top intelligence agents scrutinizing every member of his father's cabinet. Time and again, his people reported hearing stories and plans, but no one could pinpoint with whom the heretical campaign to seize neighboring St. Michel was originating.

Again, he noticed how her dark blue eyes became shadowed with what looked to him to be suspicion. For the life of him, he couldn't figure out what he'd said to make her look so guarded. He'd only told the honest truth. The edict of male-only rule *was* idiotic.

Ariane's eyes lowered to her plate. "Even if my father hadn't been involved in the marriage that left me illegitimate, and even if females could reign St. Michel, I'd never be that ruler." The corners of her mouth pulled back. "I'm second born, you know. I ave an older sister." The sigh she expelled was purosefully melodramatic. "It's like that phrase 'always a bridesmaid...never a bride.'"

Her chuckle seemed lighthearted enough to have Etienne figuring he'd misconstrued her doubtful exression of a moment before. He felt warmth creep ver him and he smiled.

"Somehow," he told her, "I don't see that old adge fitting you at all."

Ariane had never experienced confusion to this deree. One moment, Etienne seemed like a knight in hining armor ready to sweep her away from the sad eality of her life. Then out of the blue, he talked bout the devastation St. Michel was surely headed or.

Had the comment been an innocent opinion? Or ad he finally slipped up and revealed his true intention? The last thing she wanted right now was to discover that Etienne was behind the plot against her country. However, if that's what she learned, she sure didn't want to hide her head in the sand.

The two of them finished their breakfast and drove to Rhineland's largest lake, a landlocked body of crystal azure water. Etienne rented a boat from an old man who was fishing from a pier, and rowed them across the flat, calm lake. She lifted her face to the warmth of the sun, wishing she could remove the brick-like apprehension sitting in the pit of her belly.

Suddenly she realized that Etienne had stopped rowing and she dipped her chin to look him in the face. Ariane felt her heartbeat flutter. Why did he have to be so gorgeous? Why did she have to be so attracted to him? Why did they have to be thrown together when her country was going through such turmoil?

She'd have loved to simply ask him if he was planning to annex St. Michel. She wished she could come right out and tell him she was working to discover who was plotting against her country.

But that was impossible.

Then she noticed the humor lighting his gray gaze.

"Now that we're in the middle of nowhere," he said, "I can tell you what's on my mind."

Ariane blinked once, her brows raising in surprise. What in the world was he about to suggest?

"I want to take this opportunity to say that I'm on to you," he said. "Not once since we left the opera last night have you made any kind of silly observation. Each and every thought and opinion you've expressed has been completely intelligent. I want it noted that I've known all along that you're not as beef-witted as you've wanted everyone—including me—to think."

His grin was captivating enough to charm the trout right out of the lake, and although panic at having been found out had the blood whooshing through her ears, she had to admit that she was beguiled. Dazzled. Enthralled. By his charm alone.

"Now," he softly continued, easing himself closer to her, "all I have to do is figure out why you'd do such a thing in the first place."

Ariane couldn't seem to think straight with him so near. Had she really discarded her mask of stupidity? Had she let down her guard so completely?

Before she was able to answer the silent queries, Etienne cupped her face between his warm, strong hands. The air seemed to heat and churn and swell with some mysterious—

No, there was nothing mysterious about what tugged at her.

Desire.

Passion.

Yearning.

As if pulled by some invisible surge of magnetic energy, Ariane felt herself leaning toward Etienne at the same time that he drew closer to her. Her gaze was riveted to his perfect mouth. The moist, swarthy skin of his full bottom lip was a shade darker than the rest of his flesh. She wanted to taste it. She wanted to feel the roughness of his whiskers against her cheek, her neck. She wanted to run her fingers through his thick hair.

When he finally did press his mouth to hers, his kiss was sweet, almost chaste. And it left her wanting more. Much more.

He whispered her name against her lips, nestled his nose up next to hers as if he wanted to inhale the very same air as she. Ariane found this to be a most sensuous act.

Etienne kissed her again, lightly. Ardor shuddered through her body from head to toe. She wanted nothing more than to surrender to it. But something made her hesitate.

Swallowing, she forced her eyes to open. She looked at the face of her handsome prince and knew that she'd never forget this moment all the days of her life. When she was a wrinkled old woman, she'd think of the time she'd run away with Prince Etienne Kroninberg of Rhineland, and she'd smile.

But now she had to think of her country. She had to remember to whom she owed her loyalty.

Her people.

Etienne could very well be the enemy, her brain silently whispered.

Gently, she inched away from him. Out of his loving embrace.

"I can't," she told him softly. "I just can't do this."

His brow furrowed, and she could clearly see that she'd wounded him with her rejection. Something in her had her saying, "Your parents have been wonderful to me since the news of my..." The rest of her thought faded. She knew he understood. "But we both know that they wouldn't approve of this. We both know that it's your job to make a good marriage. It's your job to wed a woman who can bring something good to Rhineland." A lump formed in her throat, but she forced out, "We both know I'm not that woman."

Chapter Eight

Ariane stared out the car window only vaguely aware of the lavender and wild thyme that covered the rolling hills in a carpet of dusky purple. The tomblike silence between herself and Etienne had been more than she could bear so she'd finally reached down and snapped on the radio. Anything, even the babble of a news broadcast, was better than this unsettling quiet.

She'd messed up something terrible over the past eighteen hours or so. Dropped her guard. Completely blown her cover. When she and Etienne had escaped from the opera last night, she'd peeled off the simpleton costume she'd so painstakingly designed over the weeks since arriving in Rhineland.

It would be nice if she could blame absentmindedness for this blunder. However, she was too practical to lie to herself. Sitting here now she had to admit that each and every time she'd led Etienne to believe her brain was made of nothing more substantial than air bubbles, she'd been appalled down to the soles of her feet! She'd hated him thinking she was a brainless wonder. So now he knew she wasn't a complete idiot.

When he'd gleefully exclaimed that he'd suspected all along that she was putting on a show, she'd actually had to tamp down her joy. The elation that had shot through her was just one more indication of how much Etienne had come to mean to her. However, that delight had died a quick death just as soon as he'd expressed his determination to discover just why she'd do such a thing. The last thing she wanted was for him to learn that she'd been using him in order to spy on his government.

Making him privy to what intelligence she did have hadn't been the only way she'd blown her cover. In telling him that she wasn't the woman for him, she'd pretty much destroyed the disguising motive she'd been using for visiting his country. That was not to say that her masquerade had been going all that well since the news of her illegitimacy had broken, but at least she'd had a small thread of an excuse to hang onto regarding why she'd remained in Rhineland when everyone fully expected her to return to St. Michel in disgrace.

Now, even that thin thread had snapped by her own hand. She'd have no recourse but to return to her homeland. And she'd be leaving with very little evidence to present to the St. Michel security force. Luc Dumont, head of security, would surely be disappointed when he learned that she couldn't point a finger at who was plotting to take over their country.

Even with all this turmoil spinning in her mind,

unwittingly, she darted a quick glance at Etienne's tight profile. It should be deemed against the law for a man to be so attractive.

Again, contradictory emotions roiled inside.

No one had ever affected her the way this man had. He'd ignited something in her. A light. No—*a fire.*

A flame that flared brightly, burned white-hot.

She wouldn't regret the weeks she'd spent with him. Yet at the same time, she was relieved that she was being forced to go home. She was calmed by the knowledge that she was through with all this game playing.

Not one to toy with anyone's feelings or affections, she was content that her stint as a spy was over. Ariane frowned when the radio newscaster's report caught her attention.

"...it is not known if Prince Etienne went off willingly with the ex-princess of St. Michel or if Ariane de Bergeron kidnapped him. The royal spokesperson stated today that King Giraud plans to hold a press conference this afternoon just as soon as Luc Dumont, director of St. Michel's security force, arrives at Kroninberg Palace. The royal spokesman went on to say that rumors of Queen Laurette's collapse are true. But he rejected the suggestion that it was due to the fact that her son had gone missing. The royal physician is currently at the palace. For BBC news, this is—"

Etienne turned off the radio.

All Ariane could think to do was whisper, "I'm so sorry, Etienne. Your mother has—"

"It's hype," he stated, slicing through her sentence with his knife-sharp words. "The media are sensationalizing this thing. I talked to my father. He knows I'm fine. He'll alert your security people.''

''But they just said the queen collapsed,'' she couldn't help pointing out.

''Yes, I heard that.''

She knew that a rush of stress was to blame for his sudden brusqueness. In an effort to assuage his anxiety, she said, ''I'm sorry if I've caused your family any harm. Bad press is one thing, but if your mother has taken ill because of something I've done—'' She broke off the sentence and simply shook her head.

Intensity turned his eyes to slate-gray. ''If something's happened to my mother, it's health related. You had nothing to do with it, I assure you.''

She remembered then that he'd told her Queen Laurette had been gravely ill with pneumonia prior to Ariane's arrival in Rhineland.

For some reason, Etienne's reassurance didn't lighten the load that seemed to fall on her shoulders like a wet woolen cloak. She'd caused the royal family of Rhineland enough trouble for one visit, she gloomily surmised. First, the news of her father's teen marriage had hit the newspapers, radio and television broadcasts while she was visiting the king and queen's home. The Rhineland media had had a field day with the fact that an illegitimate princess was trying to sink her claws into their one and only son. And now those sharks of the media were in a feeding frenzy over the fact that she may or may not have kidnapped the crown prince of Rhineland.

Everyone—the king and queen, Etienne, even the Rhinelanders themselves—would be much better off if she were to go away.

Far, far away.

* * *

She'd expected to meet confusion when they arrived at the palace, but what she saw when she entered the elegant royal reception parlor would have been better described as unqualified pandemonium.

A group of diplomats, several from Rhineland and at least four from St. Michel that Ariane could recognize, were shouting, facial veins bulging on some, others waving their arms in anger. Servants scurried silently in and out of the room, bringing the ambassadors various messages, carrying refreshment, or hovering discreetly in case their services were needed. A mob of security personnel from both countries was working with electrical technicians in setting up what looked to be a center of operations complete with several pieces of high-tech computer hardware, a recording device and two telephones.

The king was not in attendance. Neither was the queen. The absence of Etienne's parents concerned Ariane to a huge degree. She could see that Etienne was experiencing an identical reaction.

"I'm sure you wouldn't mind excusing me while I go find my father," he murmured in her ear.

"Of course."

The stiff, formal nod they exchanged brought Ariane's mood another notch lower than it already was.

When she next glanced up, her gaze connected with Luc Dumont's vivid blue one. She could tell from the expression on his face that he was not happy with her.

The other men didn't even look up from their work when Luc left the group and came directly to Ariane.

"What's that all about?" she asked him lightly, pointing to the control center being set up and hoping against hope that she could lighten Luc's stern disposition. She rallied a smile as she quipped, "Did everyone honestly expect me to be calling in a ransom demand for the prince? I know I've been known to do some crazy things in my day, Luc, but..."

The man didn't crack a smile. "You know it's common procedure to prepare ourselves for any situation. The king did tell us he'd heard from his son early this morning. But that was hours ago, Ariane. We had no way of knowing what could have happened to the two of you. You could have met with—"

"Some extremely nefarious characters. Yes, you've warned me a hundred times over the years." Ariane forced another smile, but still Luc's mouth remained stubbornly grim. Finally, her shoulders sagged and she muttered, "Anyone ever tell you that you take your job much too seriously, Dumont?"

His lips pressed together in an obvious effort to suppress a hint of humor. "Yes," he answered unhesitatingly. "You." The glint in his eye was the only other signal that the gravity he was conveying was softening.

Now that his irritation had abated somewhat, Ariane felt safe to offer her heartfelt apology for slipping away without telling anyone. Tilting her head, she looked up into his face. "Would you believe that this was all Etienne's idea?"

The doubt in Luc's blue eyes told her that her long, adventure-loving reputation was going to have her shouldering the blame for this fiasco no matter what the truth of the situation really was.

At that moment, one of the St. Michel diplomats shouted, "We will not agree to issuing any kind of formal apology until it is certain Ariane de Bergeron returns unharmed and it is learned that she is at fault.''

Ariane sighed. Even her own government was willing to allow her to take responsibility for this mess.

''Gentlemen.''

Although Luc hadn't raised his tone, Ariane plainly saw that he commanded the attention of the entire room. The hubbub ceased and all eyes turned to him.

''As you can see,'' he told them, ''Ariane and the prince have returned, safe and sound.''

However, it was clear that the men weren't going to give up their argumentative attitudes easily.

''I don't see Prince Etienne.'' The Rhineland diplomat's tone was heavy with suspicion.

''What has she done with him?'' another asked. ''That woman should be taken into custody.''

A flash of fear arrowed through Ariane, and she felt an overwhelming compulsion to defend herself. ''But Etienne is fine,'' she insisted. ''He was just with me. Luc saw him. So did everyone standing around the doorway here.'' She indicated the nearby servants. ''He went to find his father, and to check on his mother.''

Only after Luc and two of the domestics had proclaimed Ariane to be telling the truth did the Rhineland dignitaries back down.

Acute awkwardness fell over everyone in the room, and it seemed that no one knew quite what to do now that the emergency had passed. Luc told his men to break down and pack up the communications center they had been setting up. Then he said to Ariane, ''Would you mind coming with me? We need to talk.'' To the dignitaries in the room, he said, ''I need to debrief Ms. de Bergeron. We won't be long.''

Once they were alone in the library, Luc gently chided, "What were you thinking, Ariane? Going off like that was—"

"But I'm okay," she said. "You didn't have to come running to my rescue."

Frustration had Luc lifting his hands, palms up. "Slipping away from security in St. Michel is one thing, but to do so on foreign soil, not to mention the fact that you were working undercover. For me. Is it any wonder that I flew here just as soon as—"

"But it really *was* Etienne's idea," she interrupted, hoping to put him at ease. Then she sighed. "I realize it was foolish of me to have agreed to go along with him." She tilted her head, her face screwing up as she explained, "But his parents took me to the opera, Luc. *The opera.* When Etienne suggested we escape the dull evening, I just couldn't resist."

She hoped her dire tone would convey to him her dilemma—and her need to flee. She knew he did when one corner of his mouth tipped up and he simply shook his head in silence.

"What can you tell me about Queen Laurette's condition?" she asked, unable to quell her concern any longer.

"We haven't been given very much information." Luc reached up to worry his chin between his thumb and index finger. "Apparently, she's fallen ill. But the doctor won't say yet if she's having a relapse of pneumonia or if it's her heart. If it was truly serious," he finally surmised, "they'd have taken her to hospital."

Common sense alone told her that much was true. Still, concern knitted Ariane's brow. Lowering her eyelids, she whispered a quick, silent prayer for good health for Etienne's mother.

The moment she opened her eyes, Luc said, "You need to return home."

"I'm ready." Ariane realized that she'd answered too quickly and concisely when she saw Luc's gaze narrow, but thankfully he kept his curiosity in check.

"I'll arrange for you to say your goodbyes to the royal family."

"That won't be necessary." She kept her tone firm.

"But protocol dictates—"

"Luc," she softly asserted, "I no longer need to concern myself with protocol."

Again, Luc looked at her askance, but remained silent.

She sighed. "Etienne and his father need to be with Queen Laurette. This is not the time for me to be bothering them with silly goodbyes."

Ariane's throat felt desert dry. She didn't want to face Etienne. Everything that needed to be said had been said out there on that lake earlier today.

"I'll send them all personal thank-you notes the moment I arrive home." Meaning to veer him away from asking any uncomfortable questions, she composed herself, nonchalantly tucked a wayward strand of hair behind her ear and asked, "How is everyone at home, anyway? Marie-Claire? Jacqueline? Has anyone heard from Lise? Wilhelm left her and has requested a divorce from King Gir—"

"Slow down. I'll tell you all the news." Luc took a seat on the overstuffed russet armchair and motioned for Ariane to sit on the adjacent couch. As soon as she was settled, he continued, "Marie-Claire and Jacqueline are fine. So is your grandmother. Everyone is staying out of Celeste's way." His jaw tightened. "That woman is turning into a veritable shrew. She's flying into rages at the least little thing."

"Has she produced the results to those DNA tests?"

"No. But those results aren't as critical as they used to be."

Ariane gasped. "You've learned something about my father's firstborn child."

"I have," Luc admitted. "I discovered that Katie Graham, King Philippe's first wife, gave birth to a boy. Your half brother."

"But this is wonderful, Luc." Joy rushed through her. "That means that—"

"Rhineland can't annex St. Michel."

Ariane felt utterly weak with relief. Her grin couldn't have gotten any bigger.

"Well," Luc said, "that is *if* I can find Philippe's son. And if he's willing to take on the job of ruling a country." He chuckled. "I can't imagine any man turning down that job, can you?"

She shook her head. This news couldn't have been better.

"Katie Graham, or Katherine as she was better known," Luc continued, "was killed in an automobile crash." Before hope could flicker in Ariane about having her title reinstated, he added, "After your father's marriage to Johanna. So your parent's union never was legitimate, Ariane. I'm sorry. However, your father's first wife died before he married Helene, so that means that Jacqueline's royal title has been restored."

Joy rushed through Ariane on her youngest sister's behalf.

Luc's gaze flattened. "Of course this validates Celeste's marriage to Philippe, as well. It also justifies her claims that her unborn child could be the heir to St. Michel's throne. But only if Katherine Graham's child can't be located. Finding your father's first son is top priority. He'd be thirty-two now.'' He grew pensive, seeming to mull over his thoughts. ''I only hope I can find him.''

''You'll find him,'' she insisted. ''I have faith in you. What more did you find out?''

''Well, before her death Katherine married an American by the name of Ellsworth Johnson. I've turned over documents to Prime Minister Davoine that prove all these facts.''

Ariane trusted Rene Davoine, St. Michel's prime minister. He'd continue with the search of the de Bergeron missing heir no matter what Celeste had to say about it.

''So I guess the documents you dug up prove that Sebastian LeMarc isn't my father's son.''

''Exactly,'' Luc told her.

''Claudette's claims were pretty outlandish from the beginning.'' Ariane shook her head. ''That she befriended my father's first wife, took her in and housed her until her baby was born. That Katie Graham returned to Texas without her child. That Claudette raised the boy. And that the boy was Sebastian. Truth is often stranger than fiction, but come on.''

Luc shrugged. ''We had to take the story seriously. That birth certificate Claudette produced sure looked legit.''

''Poor Sebastian,'' Ariane said on a sad sigh. ''He must have been left reeling. Having been told that the people you'd always thought were your parents weren't, and that you were next in line to be king...''

She exhaled in a rush. "He had to have been bowled over."

Luc nodded. "He was. But all is well now. And I have good news. News that will make you want to pack your bags and head home to St. Michel."

Ariane's brow lifted in interest.

Luc's face lit up with pleasure. "Marie-Claire and Sebastian have, er...how can I say this delicately...taken a shine to each other. They're getting married. Immediately."

"You're kidding! My youngest sister never mentioned a word when I spoke with her on the phone." Ariane knew she'd have to think up some kind of devious punishment for the ornery Marie-Claire who had so callously left her in the dark. Then she realized what all this meant. "We're going to have a wedding! Grandmama must be thrilled, I'm sure."

Remembering the plight of her oldest sister, Ariane asked, "What of Lise? She's home, isn't she? Is she okay?"

"Lise is fine. And she's home. In St. Michel."

Luc's expression grew hooded.

"What?" Panic washed over Ariane. "What is it?"

"It's just that Celeste has become petty, almost unbalanced these days. No one can predict what she might do next." He shook his head, admitting, "She's refused to allow Lise to move back into the palace."

"Marie-Claire did tell me that." Concern knit Ariane's brow. "Lise is pregnant. And surely she's feeling depressed about Wilhelm leaving her. And she's scared, I'm sure, about the future. Lise needs to be near her family. How can Celeste force her to live by herself right now? The woman really is a witch."

He heaved a sigh. "It's not really all that bad. Lise is living in a cottage on the palace grounds. She's safe and warm and dry."

"Poor thing." Ariane's ire ruffled when she thought about her stepmother's treatment of her sister. "Celeste would have us all out on our ears if she could."

Softly, Luc said, "I'm afraid you're right."

She asked about her stepsiblings, Georges and Juliet.

"Georges is great. He's doing what he can to hold down the fort. And Juliet—"

Hmmm...the way his eyes misted over, Ariane thought, one would be led to believe that Luc had some real sentimental feelings for Juliet.

"—she's fine as well."

But the smile that shadowed the corners of his mouth continued to rouse Ariane's curiosity.

After a moment of silence, he asked, "What have you found out during your visit? Did you learn who might be plotting against us?"

Her brow wrinkled and agitation had her sitting up straighter on the couch. "Making everyone think I'm a blubbering fool was a great way to get people to disclose information to me that they might not normally. They thought I was too stupid to understand the ins and outs of government. I've heard bits and pieces of gossip. Prime Minister Schmidt made some very cagey remarks about governments needing to follow the laws of their forefathers. And I heard that a man by the name of Berg Dekker is complaining long and loud about paying fees to use St. Michel's docks. I know it's not much. I'm sure there's a faction within the Rhineland government who want to seize

St. Michel, but..." She let the rest of her thought fade as she absently worried her thumb back and forth across the opposite palm.

Before she could subdue her tongue, words began to tumble from her mouth. "During the weeks I've been here," she said, "I've gotten to know Etienne pretty well. He's a formidable man. He's going to make a great ruler once his father decides to step down. But I just can't see him taking possession—taking *hostile* possession—of St. Michel. He's just too—"

"Whoa. Hold on, Ariane." Luc reached over and discreetly placed a calming hand on her knee. "When you came here, we had no one on our list of suspects. And that remains the case. No one believes that Etienne—"

He stopped, his back straightening. His eyes narrowed suddenly. "Oh, my," he softly whispered, reclining against the chair back. "I think the prince has stolen your heart."

The fact that someone other than herself was privy to her secret had a lump rising up in her throat. She had difficulty breathing, and sudden, hot tears splintered her vision into a thousand shards of light. Her chin trembled.

Displaying this kind of emotion was taboo according to all the training she'd received. A royal never let people see her cry. Ariane was a complete disgrace to the de Bergeron name.

Well, what did it matter? She wasn't a legal de Bergeron, anyway. Still, she should try to show a bit of dignity. This kind of pitiful exhibition would surely make Luc uncomfortable.

But to the contrary, the head of St. Michel's security force rose to his feet and came to sit next to her. He even put a comforting arm around her shoulders. It was then she realized that this strong, protective man would make some woman a great husband someday.

"It'll be okay, Ariane," he crooned. "Just because things look bad at the moment doesn't mean that this situation will be in the forefront of the news forever. There will be other catastrophes. Soon someone else's misfortune will take the limelight off of you and Lise and Marie-Claire. You'll see."

"Don't feed me a bunch of fairy tales, Luc." A teardrop scalded its way down Ariane's cheek. "No matter where the limelight shines next, the fact remains that my sisters and I have been proved illegitimate. *Illegitimate.* No titled man will have anything to do with us. Look at Lise. Her husband left her without a backward glance."

"Yes," he whispered, "but look at Marie-Claire. She found a good man who loves her. You will, too."

But she didn't want just any man. She wanted Etienne. But the loss of her title meant that they could never be together. Never.

Pure agony swelled in her chest. If she didn't get out of this room she'd end up sobbing like a big baby. And that wouldn't be fair to Luc. His job was to protect her, not mend her broken heart.

She pushed herself to a stand. "I've got to find Francie so we can pack. I want to go home, Luc. I want to go home now."

Chapter Nine

"It was a beautiful wedding, wasn't it?" Francie leaned closer to the mirror and applied powder to her forehead and chin with small, quick pats.

"It was," Ariane agreed. "Marie-Claire looked lovely in grandmother's wedding dress. All that white satin and chiffon. She looked like she was floating down the aisle. And there must have been a hundred tiny buttons. Just gorgeous."

Lise had worn Simone's wedding dress when she'd married Wilhelm. And Marie-Claire had worn it today. A tinge of sadness shot through Ariane when she realized that her chance to wear her grandmother's gown would surely never come.

Then she turned her attention to her half sister, Jacqueline. "And you, my sunshine, made a beautiful candle lighter."

The twelve-year-old wrinkled her nose prettily. "I tried to tell Marie-Claire that I'm old enough to be a real bridesmaid.'' She exhaled a long-suffering sigh. ''But she just wouldn't listen.''

An affectionate smile was Ariane's only response. Jacqueline had been lodging that same complaint for the full two weeks that Marie-Claire had been planning her wedding.

''Would you look at that,'' Francie commented. ''The child is cute even when she pouts.''

''Oh, Francie,'' Jacqueline grumbled. ''I am not.''

Ariane laughed. ''You are, too,'' she insisted, planting a kiss on her youngest sister's forehead.

Laughter and smiles on the outside. That's what Ariane had strived for. She desperately wanted to cover the turmoil continuing to rage inside her.

Ever since her return to St. Michel, Ariane hadn't experienced a single moment when thoughts of Etienne weren't hovering around somewhere in her head. She often visited with her older sister Lise at the cottage, offering her comfort, an ear, and many days a sturdy shoulder to cry on. Ariane had thrown herself into the wedding preparations, going to seemingly endless dress fittings, attending rehearsals, helping to choose music and shopping with Marie-Claire and her other sisters, full, half and step, as all the females eagerly offered opinions as the bride picked out her trousseau.

But on the inside Ariane had felt like an automaton. A walking zombie.

She wanted to be a good and strong presence for all her sisters so she did all she could to hide the sadness that filled her. Thankfully, Marie-Claire was too much in love, too preoccupied with wedding plans to notice the agony Ariane was feeling. And Lise, pregnant and alone, had too many worries of her own and was doing what she could to allow Marie-Claire the attention she deserved at this most happy time. In fact, everyone at the palace seemed caught up in the festivities.

Except for Celeste. Ariane's stepmother spent her days vacillating between agitation, grumpiness and out-and-out anger. But despite the woman's bouts of ranting, the de Bergeron sisters had banded together to throw together a beautiful wedding for Marie-Claire.

However, even in the face of the joyous occasion Ariane had felt stiff as a board and utterly emotionless as she'd walked down the aisle.

Until she saw him.

Etienne had been in the church this afternoon.

Her step had faltered when their eyes met. And held.

Always a bridesmaid, never a bride, she'd recalled telling him.

Somehow I don't think that old adage fits you at all, she'd remembered him replying.

She had departed Rhineland knowing that she'd left her heart behind—in Etienne's possession. But as the two of them stared at one another in the dimly lit church, Ariane realized the depth of her love for her prince. Etienne had done more than win her heart—he'd captured her very soul.

Knowing that nothing could ever come of the love that filled her to the brim had been devastating to her. Luckily, she'd been able to garner enough of her wits together to complete her trek down the aisle. But she'd barely heard a word of the ceremony, she had been quaking so terribly inside.

"You're a beautiful bridesmaid." Young Jacqueline smoothed her hand over her sister's loose, shoulder-length hair, pulling Ariane back into the here and now.

"Thank you, love."

Always a bridesmaid. That phrase would always have a poignant memory attached to it, Ariane realized.

She blinked, thinking once again of the intensity of Etienne's pewter gaze as he'd stared at her in the church earlier. If she hadn't known better, she'd be compelled to believe he was trying to communicate some profound message to her.

Foolish woman, a silent voice scorned.

Always a bridesmaid. Again, the axiom whispered through her mind.

Yes, that's just what she'd be.

Just then the door opened and the dowager queen entered the powder room. "Is this a private party? Or can anyone join?"

"Grandmama!" Jacqueline jumped up from the dainty stool and raced to the elderly lady. Simone met the child's warm enthusiasm with open arms.

"I can't wait," Jacqueline said to the elderly woman, "to get my chance to borrow your wedding dress."

"And you'll make a lovely bride. But you must give yourself time to grow up first." Simone's smile shined love down on her youngest granddaughter. "You were fabulous today, my dear. I'm very proud of you."

"Thank you," Jacqueline said primly.

Ariane's mouth quirked when she noticed that her young half sister didn't repeat her objection about being old enough to be a bridesmaid. Jacqueline evidently knew that complaining to Simone would warrant nothing more than a lesson in royal etiquette.

A noble never groused.

"Francie," Simone addressed Ariane's lady-in-waiting, "would you mind taking this young lady to the reception?" To Jacqueline, she said, "They've set out the dessert."

Jacqueline's eyes lit with delight, and she and Francie left the powder room.

Ariane fished a comb from her beaded bag and ran it lightly through her hair. "Marie-Claire looks lovely, doesn't she?"

Simone said, "She does. And so do you. You've always looked wonderful in deep purple. Your skin just glows."

A silent smile of thanks was Ariane's answer.

If it hadn't been for her grandmother, there had been times during her life when Ariane had thought she'd lose her mind living in this hodge-podge of a family. Simone was a loving and caring constant in what often seemed an extremely chaotic world. Of course, she was also very prim and proper, the picture of self-control.

"Or, hmmm, I wonder—" Simone's tone took on a teasing lilt "—if there could be another reason behind that glow."

Her whole body going taut, Ariane held her breath as she waited for her grandmother to offer more details. Simone didn't disappoint her.

"There's a handsome prince at the reception who seems to be on the lookout for someone." The elderly woman's face wrinkled with a soft smile. "Could it be you he's searching for?"

Ariane's heart pounded like a hammer.

"Etienne's looking for me?"

Simone beamed. "Is there another prince that you've fallen in love with?"

Unable to contain her surprised gasp, she gawked at her grandmother, knowing full well doing so was most unladylike. "But...how did you know?"

"Oh, dear child," Simone cooed, "at the ripe old age of seventy-five if I can't spot someone wearing their heart on their sleeve, then I may as well open the gate and put myself out to pasture."

Ariane's spirit plummeted. Had she really revealed her feelings for Etienne so openly in that split second of hesitation when walking down the aisle?

"You weren't the only one who was blatantly expressing your feelings." Simone's laugh was soft as goose down.

The room felt as if it were devoid of oxygen. Ariane couldn't seem to inhale, so she waited. Breathless.

"From what I could see," the elderly lady continued, "that man is just as smitten with you as you are with him."

Hope soared inside Ariane as if it had sprouted the powerful wings of eagles and taken flight. But the reality of her situation had despair weighing down the fleeting anticipation.

"Even if he does feel something for me," Ariane said, unable to get her voice above a whisper, "nothing could ever come of it. He's the crown prince of Rhineland. I'm just—"

"A kind, caring and clever young woman with plenty to offer," Simone asserted stubbornly. "Not to mention the fact that you're terrifically beautiful to boot."

Ariane fell silent, not knowing how to respond. She loved that her grandmother would come to her defense so fiercely. But reality was what it was. And there could be no changing it.

As if tuned into Ariane's thoughts, Simone's brows arched regally. "My dear, do not underestimate the power of love. It can move mountains. Just look at what it did for Marie-Claire and Sebastian." Gazing off, Simone reached up, lightly touching her index finger to her lips as she suddenly became lost in thought. Finally, she said, "Words can't express how happy I am that she married for love."

It was common knowledge that Simone's marriage to Ariane's grandfather, Antoine de Bergeron, had been an arranged one.

"Oh, I'm not complaining," Simone continued softly. "Antoine and I grew to love each other over the years." She grinned at Ariane. "But in the beginning, things were pretty rocky. The love Marie-Claire and Sebastian share will save them that much, at least."

The warmth of her grandmother's velvet touch on her shoulders had Ariane meeting Simone's gentle gaze.

"You don't look convinced that love is a mighty force."

A knot of emotion swelled in Ariane's throat until it actually grew painful. "Oh, what I feel for Etienne is powerful, all right." She sighed. "But I feel so guilty. I've wronged him, you know. I've wronged him in more ways than one."

Simone didn't speak and loving patience seemed to palpitate from her as she waited for Ariane to unburden herself.

"First off, I misjudged him terribly. All those months ago when he first showed an interest in me, I was angry that Father seemed to be forcing Etienne on me. Father seemed determined to make a union between the de Bergeron and the Kroninberg houses, and it infuriated me that I was his bait. Pure stubbornness had me believing a bunch of preconceived notions about Etienne. I convinced myself I wouldn't like him. Surely he was boring, I thought. Surely he was stuffy. Surely he was high-minded. Not the kind of man who would interest me at all. But what I took for arrogance, wasn't arrogance at all, Grandmama. It was a seriousness regarding who and what he was—a prince with a future filled with duty and responsibility.

"And I wronged him, too," she continued, "by suspecting he was behind the plot to seize St. Michel. I have no rock-hard evidence that he isn't involved, I just know in my heart that he's not the kind of man who would do something so ruthless."

Her grandmother smoothed a satiny hand down Ariane's cheek. "Follow your heart, child. Listen to what it tells you and you'll never be led astray."

Agony had tears springing to Ariane's eyes. "But my heart is telling me to go to Etienne right now. To tell him how I feel, title or no title. And all that will do is force him to reject me."

"There you go again," Simone tenderly chastised, shaking her head. "Underestimating."

There was that hope again. New wings budding to life.

Ariane blinked. "You really think I should go to him?" Anxiety wrinkled her brow. "But won't he think I'm...forward?"

Simone waved away Ariane's fears. "This is a new age, my dear. These days, women go after what they want."

In that instant, Ariane felt light as air. Almost buoyant.

What do you have to lose? a silent voice soughed through her mind.

Nothing. And everything.

Fear clawed at her.

What do you really *have to lose?* the voice insisted.

Well—Ariane's mind whirled like a dervish—if she revealed her heart to him, he could politely turn her down, using his princely duty as a perfectly acceptable excuse. However, if she were to reveal her feelings for him…he just might take her in his arms and tell her he felt the same way.

The attraction that had hummed between them like an electric current couldn't be denied. By either of them.

But if she didn't bare her soul to him, she would spend the rest of her life wondering what Etienne's response might have been. Could she live with that regret for the remainder of her days?

She knew that simply wasn't an option.

Her decision made, she couldn't keep the smile from her lips as she said to her grandmother, "I want you to know I love you. And I'll be forever grateful to you for urging me to—"

Simone silenced her with a soft index finger against her lips, her eyes shining as brightly as Ariane's.

"You're wasting time, my child. Go get that man and make him yours."

Giving her grandmother's hand a quick squeeze, Ariane raced from the room to seek her destiny.

Whatever fate had in store, regret over remaining silent about her love for Etienne wouldn't have a part in it.

The quick loop she'd made around the reception hall hadn't turned up her prince. Ariane's gaze darted from face to face. She had to find him. He couldn't possibly have left without seeing her, could he?

Suddenly, she came upon Luc and Juliet. The couple looked positively secreted away in the secluded niche and they parted as soon as they saw her. Was that guilt she felt emanating from them? But her mind was too preoccupied to give the matter much thought.

"Have you seen Prince Etienne?" she asked them.

"He was asking for you earlier," Juliet said.

The ever-vigilant Luc replied, "I saw him go outside. Toward the gardens."

Of course. The formal gardens. Why hadn't she thought to look there rather than become panicked that Etienne might have taken his leave without saying goodbye?

"Thank you," Ariane said to Juliet and Luc, and then she rushed toward the wide, arched stone doorway that led to the gardens.

The pungent scent of pine mingled with the aroma of hyacinth and lupine as she made her way along the pea-stone path that winded through the trees, shrubs and blooming bulbs. The setting sun had turned the horizon a vivid burnt orange, but Ariane barely noticed it.

She called his name just as soon as she'd caught sight of him.

He turned to face her, and she couldn't keep herself from running the final steps that separated them.

That familiar throbbing vibration resonated, thick and heavy, in the silent moments they spent studying each other. She felt as if she hadn't seen him in months.

Tell him, her brain screeched at her. *Tell him all you feel.*

I will, I will, she silently promised herself. But she was trembling so. With elation. With fear.

Taking a deep calming breath, she decided at last to take it slow. Her dream, her fairy tale, her idea of *rapturous paradise* would begin—or end—tonight. The perfect words would have to be carefully chosen.

"How is your mother?" she asked softly, feeling suddenly shy. "Recuperating well, I hope."

The small smile he offered her spoke of his gratitude that she cared enough about his mother to ask after her health.

"She's improving daily," he told her. "She and my father send their regrets for being unable to attend your sister's wedding. But my mother simply must follow doctor's orders."

"Of course." The air felt so...warm. "It was kind of you to attend in their stead."

He murmured, "I wouldn't have missed it." His gray eyes leveled on her. "I'm sorry we had to part without saying a proper goodbye, and I appreciated the note you sent. In fact—" he deftly slipped his fingers between the facings of his jacket and extracted the ivory envelope "—I've read it at least a thousand times."

Ariane's heart fluttered furiously against her ribs. He'd kept her note. On his person. He'd read it again and again. That had to mean something wonderful...didn't it?

Emotions waged a war inside her. She wanted to trust her intuition, but the panic over misconstruing his meaning was rising like the swell of a great and potentially fatal tidal wave.

Awkwardness had her gaze sliding from his. "I've been so busy since I returned home."

"I understand," he told her, tension pulling his tone taut. "Helping your sister plan her wedding, I'm sure." After a heady pause, he haltingly declared, "It was a beautiful wedding."

He'd strung out the word beautiful, emphasizing it, and that had Ariane's eyes latching onto his once again.

Had that compliment really been meant for her? Was he implying that he thought her beautiful?

Oh, she wished that if that were so, he'd come right out and speak his mind. It certainly would make her intentions of revealing her feelings for him a little less frightening.

"I've been busy, too," he told her.

"Oh?"

Etienne nodded. "With Mother so ill, I've been fulfilling Father's obligations."

He grinned then, and she thought her heart would melt right down into her shoes by how appealing she found it.

"And I had to make my own travel arrangements," he continued. "Seems I'm about to lose my equerry."

"Harry is leaving his post?" she asked.

Etienne nodded. "Seems he's about to ask your lady-in-waiting to marry him. Harry approached Francie's father to ask permission and the man not only granted it, he also asked Harry to come work for him."

Placing her palm against the purple satin bodice of her gown, Ariane released a poignant sigh. "Oh, Francie must be ecstatic. I wonder why she hasn't told me? That woman couldn't keep a secret if her life depended on it."

"She hasn't told you because she doesn't know yet."

Happiness for her friend had Ariane smiling warmly. "I won't say a word. I'd never dream of bursting her bubble."

Do not underestimate the power of love. It can move mountains.

Her grandmother's words gurgled through her mind like a fountain of fresh spring water.

Follow your heart, child. Listen to what it tells you and you'll never be led astray.

Still, fear of rejection paralyzed her tongue. But then her mind was bombarded with all of Etienne's kindnesses: he had done everything he could to save her from humiliation after Wilhelm had sold the story of the de Bergeron scandal to the media, and in the weeks that followed Etienne had insisted that everyone treat her with respect. She also recalled how he'd taken her away from that boring old opera, and how he'd shown her such a wonderful time at Byron Falls. He was a good man. A caring man. And she loved him. Down to the very soul of her being.

She swallowed and garnered every ounce of her courage. "There's something I want you to know."

His gaze glistened with curiosity, and Ariane was certain she observed a keen anticipation in his handsome face.

Footsteps crunching on the pea-stone path had both

Ariane and Etienne turning to see Celeste approaching.

At nearly eight months pregnant, the woman's belly protruded under the pale yellow chiffon. Ariane had wanted to warn her stepmother that yellow wasn't a good color for blondes, that it turned the skin tone pallid, but Celeste had been so on edge lately that Ariane knew the woman would have misinterpreted the advice as pure criticism. So, she had simply kept her opinion to herself.

While Ariane and her sisters had been helping Marie-Claire plan her wedding, they had all steered clear of their stepmother. Celeste had flatly refused to allocate funds for something as frivolous as Marie-Claire's nuptials. Why, the woman had proclaimed for everyone to hear, the three daughters of Johanna Van Rhys weren't even real royalty. In Celeste's opinion, a grand wedding was not necessary.

Of course, the sisters had disagreed. Marie-Claire had spent her life as a princess, Ariane had thought, so she deserved a day of splendor...even if it was on a small scale.

Now, Celeste's eyes narrowed with unmistakable nastiness. "Well, my, my...what have we here?" she purred like a spiteful cat. She raked Ariane up and down with a scathing glance. "Don't tell me the middle by-blow thinks she's going to snag herself a prince."

Chapter Ten

Her knees went wobbly and dizziness swam in her head. Ariane heard the tiny, far off mew of a weak kitten, and then was overwhelmed with a dark conglomeration of amazement, confusion and anxiety when she realized that the sound had bubbled up from her own throat.

"Do you honestly believe he would want the likes of you?" Celeste's voice sliced to the bone. "He has everything. Land. Money. Status. A kingdom will someday be his. But you…you can offer him nothing. You have nothing. You *are* nothing."

Each slur was like a physical slap in the face. Mortification was too mild a word to describe what was crashing through her like a rock slide. Her stepmother couldn't have hurt her more if she'd taken a rapier and run her clean through. How could Celeste humiliate her so? And in front of Etienne? But the even bigger question was…why would she do this? *Why?*

She and her stepmother had never had the best of

relationships. But then Celeste hadn't bonded with any of King Philippe's children or stepchildren. She simply didn't waste her time with anyone who couldn't offer her something she needed or wanted. And it didn't help that she was a jealous woman. She'd been resentful of Philippe's love for the children living under his roof, she'd been envious of any attention he gave them.

However, the behavior she was flaunting now seemed very strange, indeed. Although she was a woman who, when wronged, would go out of her way to exact revenge, she didn't normally sink her fangs into someone who hadn't injured her in some way.

For Celeste to bombard her with such a degrading attack—with no provocation—just didn't make sense. No sense at all.

Suddenly, Ariane realized she was being propped up by a mass that was warm. Solid. Strong. As if she were moving through a thick, viscous fog, she tilted her head and looked up to find Etienne standing beside her, one arm curled protectively around her shoulders.

"With all due respect, *Your Highness*—"

The manner in which he'd twisted the formal address was clear indication that he was offering the current queen of St. Michel anything but respect.

"There's more to royalty than mere chance of birth."

Ariane tipped up her chin further to get a better look at Etienne who was glaring at Celeste. His facial muscles were taut, his dark brows bunching with the fury that so obviously rolled through him.

"Royalty is synonymous with dignity," he continued. "Goodness. Nobility. These qualities are innate in the aristocracy. They come from within.

"Royalty isn't worn on the outside." The calmness in his tone didn't take the bite out of his words, and his opinion was exemplified by the fact that he took a moment to let his gaze wander over the strand upon strand of expensive pearls draped around her neck, the chunky gold rings flashing with emeralds and rubies that adorned her fingers.

Ariane had never seen his eyes so cold and flat, like dull steel.

"Royalty," he continued, "can't be acquired through marriage."

Celeste's face went ghost white and she was barely able to contain the gasp that rose to her crimson lips. Ariane was certain her stepmother was about to fall to her knees from shock right there on the garden path.

Etienne couldn't have injured Celeste more even if he'd physically struck her. Evidently, he was privy to her past...he must know of her background prior to marrying Philippe.

She'd been a commoner. Not a single nobleman climbed among the branches of her family tree. She didn't even have the privilege of calling herself one of the nouveau riche. She'd simply been an average, middle-class woman chosen to be queen because she'd used her wiles to capture Philippe's eye, and then she'd wielded her powers of persuasion to convince him that she could provide the male heir that the royal house of St. Michel so desperately needed.

Celeste quickly regained her composure. Anger had her cheeks blotched with an ugly red.

Her top lip convulsed in a sneer. "I should just

keep what I know to myself,'' she said to Etienne. ''Ariane is just what you deserve.'' She smoothed her palms over her swollen waistline. ''But I'm going to prove to you how regal I can be. I'm going to forgive your nasty remarks and reveal the truth.''

Her stepmother's gaze leveled on her, chilling Ariane to the marrow.

''You thought I didn't know,'' Celeste said. ''You thought your conniving and spying was a secret. Well, there are consequences to every action, dear girl. And now you're going to face yours.''

Ariane's blood froze in her veins. Her stepmother knew that she'd been in Rhineland to spy on Etienne's government.

No, she wanted to shout at Celeste. *Please stop!* Having Etienne learn what she'd done—like this—wasn't what Ariane wanted. She'd planned to break it to him gently...*after* she'd revealed her heart to him.

Celeste turned her attention to Etienne once again. ''You may have thought Ariane was visiting your country to further develop the interest you showed in her just before my poor husband passed away. But I'm here to tell you that you've been duped.''

Feeling as if she'd been surrounded by a glass bubble, Ariane couldn't seem to draw breath. She was horrified. By the words coming out of her stepmother's mouth. By the look on Etienne's face.

''Ariane was in your country,'' the woman barreled full-steam ahead, ''acting as a spy for our security force. Word had reached us that some faction inside your government meant to annex St. Michel. Ariane's mission was to find out who was behind the plot.''

Her gaze zeroed in on him. "And *you,* Prince Etienne, were at the top of the list of suspects."

Ariane's short, sharp inhalation drew his attention. Slowly, he swiveled his head, and where—just a moment ago—that icy pewter stare had been aimed at Celeste, it was now directed on *her.*

"But that's not true," Ariane said, her tone a mere breathy whisper forced from her aching throat. Without thought, she continued, "There wasn't a list of suspects. There still isn't. Celeste, why are you doing this?"

Her stepmother's gaze was cool and collected. "What can I tell you? I am who I am. And besides that, the shrimp on the buffet table have upset my stomach. I'm feeling a little grumpy. For some strange reason, I feel that it just wouldn't be right for me to stand by and see the crown prince of Rhineland saddled with the likes of you."

After having offered the only excuse she evidently meant to give, Celeste turned on her heel and made her way back toward the wedding reception.

The funny thing was, the parting shot her stepmother had made hadn't wounded Ariane in the least. She guessed that, at that point, she was simply numb.

The hurt, the accusation, the questions radiating from Etienne's gaze forced her to lift her eyes to his.

"Is it true?"

It was such a small question. Just three little words. Yet Ariane knew the query was going to ruin what might have been.

There was so much she wanted to say. So much she wanted to explain. She couldn't answer the question he'd asked without first defending her actions. If she did, he'd resent her forever. He'd be terribly hurt, and he wouldn't hear the really important matters she had wanted to discuss.

Matters of the heart.

"Etienne, before I—"

"All I want from you," he viciously interrupted, "is the truth. Did you come to Rhineland to spy on my government?"

There was only one way for her to answer. So, after only a second's hesitation, she softly admitted, "Yes."

His jaw tensed. "And you used me to do it."

This was not a question. Still, Ariane felt compelled to nod.

"But Celeste lied when she said you were on the list of suspects," she rushed to say. "When I left home, there were no suspects."

Pain flickered in his gaze. "Do you really think that matters to me?"

Sadness welled up inside her. "I guess it doesn't."

His pain seemed to metamorphose into a deep anguish right before her eyes, and she thought her heart was going to rip into two ragged pieces.

"I've got to go," he stated, his voice hard and sharp as slivers of granite. "I must fly to Washington, DC, for my father. With Mother still so weak, he refuses to go. I'm to go in his place. I didn't want us to part again without having the chance to say goodbye." He emitted a sound much like a growl. "I've been a fool."

He'd actually taken a step away from her before she was able to get her tongue to work.

"Etienne! Please. Wait."

For an instant, she thought he meant to walk away

from her. Every muscle in her body quaked as he paused, and then he turned to stare at her in silence.

"I know everything is ruined," she told him. "I understand completely if you never want to see me again."

One moment passed. Then two.

She wanted desperately to bare her soul to him. But her fear was too strong.

But in that moment, she truly realized she had nothing to lose.

"I want you to know—" she paused long enough to moisten her lips and swallow "—that when I returned home to St. Michel…I left my heart in Rhineland. With you."

Emotion burned her eye sockets and an instant later unshed tears blurred her vision.

"I know my actions are unforgivable," she continued. "I should never have used your interest in me the way that I did. But we were desperate, Etienne. My country was in peril. You'd have done the same thing had you been in my shoes. I know it isn't much of an excuse, but the love I feel for my country…the loyalty I have for my father's subjects…those are all I have left."

His pewter eyes didn't soften a bit.

"I never expected to fall in love with you, Etienne. I never in a million years expected you to be so…kind to me. Especially after the news was out that I'd lost everything." She took her bottom lip between her teeth for a moment, pondering just how much she should say. Finally, she could hold back no longer. "Why would you be so kind, so respectful…unless you were up to something yourself? I wondered…I couldn't help but wonder, Etienne…was it possible that you were attempting to remain as close as you could to the de Bergeron throne?''

"So you did suspect me?''

His accusation cut her like a knife.

"What else was I to think?'' Her tone rose in pitch, but she immediately felt contrite. "But it didn't take me long to see that you're too good-hearted to do something as brutal as seizing a neighboring country that had been friends with yours for so many years.''

She watched his jaw muscle tense and relax, tense and relax. Time seemed to slow until her nerves fairly jittered right out of her skin.

"Now I understand the stupid act you played,'' he said. "You thought your naïveté would seem harmless...that *you* would seem harmless...while you were steadily pumping my father's government officials for information.'' The magnitude of his ire had his gaze abruptly averting to the pea-stone path. "I've got to go, Ariane. I've got to go now.''

There was a finality in those words that had tears spilling unchecked down her cheeks, her chin trembling. "You do forgive me, don't you?'' She heard the reckless urgency in her tone and didn't care one wit. "I mean, I can live with the fact that we can't be together. It wouldn't have worked anyway. No one in Rhineland would be in favor of such a union. Your parents. Your government. Your people.'' She swallowed. "You're expected to marry a woman with...''

The rest of the thought faded into oblivion. She didn't have it in her to once again list all she'd lost when she'd been labeled illegitimate.

"But, Etienne, I couldn't stand it,'' she said, heedless of the pleading stance of her body language, "if

I thought your anger over my actions was so great that you couldn't find it in your heart to forgive me.''

He was silent for some time. Finally, he said, ''I've got to go. My plane will be waiting.''

''Of course,'' she murmured, her heart rending into dozens of pieces. He was going to withhold clemency. He was going to imprison her in walls of blame. ''You have a country to represent. I understand fully.''

''I'm overwhelmed, Ariane. I'm...I'm—''

But he refused to make any further declarations that might weaken him further. She saw that much glistening in his wounded gaze.

Then he cleared his throat against the still awkwardness that had descended upon them. ''I'll be gone a few days. I'll call you when I return from the U.S.''

The desolate sound of his retreating footsteps crunching on the tiny stones as he walked away from her was something Ariane would never forget. Not in all her days.

''Sure.'' The soft spring breeze carried away her whispered response, but it couldn't remove the despair that filled her spirit. ''Sure you will.''

The minutes...the hours...the days dragged by as if something strange had happened to decelerate time itself. Ariane walked listlessly back toward the palace after having spent much of the afternoon with her oldest sister, Lise.

No matter how depressing she found the state of her own life, Ariane did her best to put on a happy optimistic front when she visited Lise. Pregnant and alone, Lise was filled with anxiety regarding the future for her and her baby.

Ariane had attempted to point out the best aspect of her sister's plight: she was free of Wilhelm, a man she'd never loved, but had married for purely political reasons in order to appease their father. However, Lise didn't seem bolstered by that fact. If the truth were to be known, Ariane fully understood. Lise was a woman alone, just as Ariane now was; however, Lise would soon have a child she would be responsible for. No wonder her sister was fraught with fear.

At least, Ariane thought, Lise had something with which to occupy her time. An expert in appraising objets d'art and jewels, Lise spent her days cataloguing all the royal artifacts owned by the de Bergeron family. In fact, Lise had shooed Ariane out of the cottage door, stating that she needed some quiet time in order to do a little research on one particular original oil painting that hung in the palace gallery.

Tramping over the hilly meadow that separated Lise's cottage from the palace, Ariane wondered what on earth she'd do with the rest of her day. A fresh breeze blew through the glossy leaves of the tree in front of her, the sun causing the foliage to wink and sparkle like metal. No. Like liquid silver.

Immediately, she was transported back in time to the moments she and Etienne had spent together at Byron Falls. They had slept together, his body protecting her from the night's chill. The intimacy she'd experienced had made her feel bonded to Etienne in a very special way. Had started her dreaming about being with him forever and always.

Ariane shoved the image and the notion from her

mind. Reaching down, she plucked a weed that seemed to strain toward the sun.

Etienne was gone from her life forever. She simply had to resign herself to that.

She wondered what she'd do with herself for the remainder of the day. She hated having so much time on her hands. Normally, she'd be out gallivanting over the countryside on a horse, or exploring St. Michel's few caves, or hiking until she was exhausted. But none of these activities seemed to interest her.

Marie-Claire was with Sebastian on his yacht as they sailed the Greek Islands on their honeymoon. Even Francie had abandoned Ariane. Her lady-in-waiting was with Harry in London meeting his family. Francie was taking a full year to plan her wedding, wanting her nuptials to be the talk of St. Michel. And if Ariane knew Francie, the wedding would be stunning.

Indulging in a bit of useless daydreaming, Ariane decided there and then that she would settle for a few loving words spoken in front of a vicar in the tiniest church in all of St. Michel.

A wedding is not in your future, a harsh voice chastised. And it was all her own fault, she knew.

Ariane tossed the weed to the ground, and shoved the thought from her brain. Love and marriage. They were nothing more than whim and fancy. Something she didn't have time for.

She nearly groaned. It seemed that time was all she did have. And time seemed bound and determined to crawl by like an itty-bitty inchworm on a journey of a thousand miles.

Movement at the crest of the hill had her squinting

against the sun. She grinned, thanking her lucky stars. Jacqueline had evidently finished her lessons and was racing to meet her. Ariane knew her youngest sister never failed to divert her attention from all these depressing thoughts of what she'd never have with Etienne.

"What's that you've got?" Ariane called once the child was close enough to hear.

"It's for you!" Jacqueline was so out of breath she could barely speak. "There's...There's—"

"Slow down." Ariane laughed at her antics. "My favorite baby sister has gone into a tizzy."

"But there's a man at the house. Waiting for you. And he brought you this."

Taking the small dish from her sister, Ariane felt the coolness of the ceramic against her palm.

"It's..."

Could she believe her eyes? Could it mean...?

"It's crème brûlé!"

So excited was she at the implication that she dropped the custard cup in the meadow and dashed up the hill toward home, the hem of her full skirt flipping up with each step.

"But what about the pudding?" Jacqueline shouted after her.

"We'll get it later. Come on, Jackie! Come on!"

By the time they reached the palace, Ariane's hair was in tangles. She was panting. And a fine sheen of perspiration made her nose shine. But she didn't care. Her only thought was to discover the identity of her visitor.

Her grandmother was just coming out of the door leading to the parlor. "I was just coming to find you." But after Simone had a chance to get a good look at her, she clicked her tongue against the roof of her mouth. "You're a mess." But as she smoothed her fingers through Ariane's hair her eyes glistened with excitement that couldn't be controlled. "You've got a visitor."

"Grandmama," Ariane breathed, the thrill she felt making her tone quake, "he brought my favorite sweet."

Simone's soft mouth spread into a smile. "Oh, he brought more than one."

Ariane's heart tripped against her ribs. He was here. And it wasn't a dream.

"Well, don't keep the man waiting," her grandmother gently chided, evidently giving up any attempt to make Ariane look more presentable.

When Jacqueline made to follow her sister into the parlor, Simone caught her by the hand. "You are coming with me, young lady. You're a mess, too. Your face needs washing and your hair needs a good brushing."

"But Ariane looks just as bad as I do—"

"Never you mind about Ariane," Simone said. "She's old enough to take care of herself."

Jacqueline groaned in a most unladylike fashion, whining, "Why do I always have to miss the good stuff?"

The child was led off toward the stairway by her grandmother. Ariane stood outside the parlor door, her mind racing. She quickly combed her fingers through the tangle of her hair, and after tucking one hopelessly knotted strand behind her ear, she hurried inside the room where the love of her life was waiting.

He stared out the window, his own agitation showing as his hands clenched and unclenched in fists behind his back.

Oh, Lord, but he was devastatingly handsome. Etienne Kroninberg was enough to melt the heart of any woman he came near. He succeeded in dissolving hers into a pulpy mass each and every time she laid eyes on him, that much was certain.

Hoping to capture his attention without having to speak, she smoothed her palms down the waistline of her skirt and shifted her weight from one foot to the other. Instinctively, he turned. And his pewter eyes were on her.

He seemed to devour her with his gaze, and Ariane felt her stomach churn with wild anticipation.

Could she be reading something into his visit, into his gift, into his eyes that wasn't really there? What about his parents? she wondered. What about his princely duty to make a good marriage? What of—

"Hello, Ariane."

The melodic sound in his greeting raised the fine hairs on her arms.

"Hello." Suddenly, she felt like a teenager meeting a boy for the first time. Timidity seemed to wrap her in a silken cocoon, but she'd be darned if she'd let it get the best of her this time.

"I brought you a gift."

She let her gaze follow where he indicated, and she gasped when she saw the trays laden with servings of crème brûlé that covered the top of not one, not two, but three of the tables in the parlor.

Laughter bubbled up from inside her. "You'll have me as fat as a cow."

"It's a bribe, you know."

Her chin dipped automatically at the sound of his

tone, and she found herself looking at him through raised lashes. "A bribe?"

She felt positively giddy with trepidation.

"I'm hoping you'll forgive me," he said. "For walking away from you at Marie-Claire's wedding without...well, without working out everything that was standing between us."

Emotion, dark and thick, flooded through her at the mention of the moment he'd walked away from her, the moment she'd been sure that all her hopes and dreams had died.

"Oh, Etienne," she said, unable to stop the words from tumbling from her lips, "I can't tell you how sorry I am about the way I hurt you."

His gaze turned a soft dove-gray and he nodded a silent acceptance of her apology.

Relief burst like a nova inside her, colorful and liberating. If his only intention in being here was to forgive her for using him the way she had, Ariane felt that would be enough.

"I shouldn't have come to Rhineland—"

"It's okay, Ariane," he said, his voice gentle and full of understanding. "You were right when you said I would have done the very same thing had my government...my homeland been threatened as yours seemed to be." He took a moment to take a deep breath. "I have my own confession to make."

The tiniest of frowns bit into the small space between her brows. What could he have to confess?

"You see," he continued, looking penitent, "I've known all along about the plot to annex St. Michel. So has my father."

Ariane couldn't contain her shock.

"Oh, we don't know who's behind the conspiracy,'' he rushed to assure her. ''But from the moment of your father's death, we've heard rumors that there were some inside our government who would like to see your country seized by our own.'' His expression took on a pained look. ''I'm sure you can understand what's behind it all. It's the port city of St. Michel. It's your access to the river...to the North Sea.''

Now it was her turn to nod in understanding. She was quite aware of why the Rhinelanders might be envious of St. Michel, even though her country was the smaller of the two.

''I've been working with the most trusted members of my intelligence force,'' he told her. ''Father and I were hoping to discover—''

''I wish you'd have told me,'' she broke in.

''I didn't want to worry you. And Father felt it might harm our relations with your country if news of this conspiracy got out. We wanted to take care of this...since we're fairly certain it's someone or some group inside our own government.''

Curiosity had her asking, ''So you haven't discovered who's behind this?''

''No. A lot of people are talking about it, but so far all we're getting is rumor and innuendo. No hard facts.''

She told him her suspicions regarding Rhineland's prime minister and the man named Berg Dekker. Ariane brightened when a thought suddenly occurred to her. ''Do you think that's all this could be? Talk? Maybe...''

She let the rest of her theory fade when she saw him shake his head.

''I believe there is a plan afoot,'' he said. ''And I'm committed to weeding out the extremists. They're planning and plotting against St. Michel. Their actions are unlawful. And I want them punished."

"You should speak with the head of our security force. Luc Dumont might be able to help you discover the identity of the people behind the scheme. In fact, I'd be happy to help, too."

He grinned then. "Well, you've sure proved that you're an excellent infiltrator."

Embarrassment heated her cheeks.

"Our governments can work together on this," he agreed. "I want these fanatics jailed as soon as possible."

St. Michel was safe. Etienne was going to see that it was. And he wasn't even connected to St. Michel's royal family or government.

The love she felt for him swelled her heart to the point of bursting.

"Why?" Her question came out in a whisper. "Why would you feel so adamant about protecting St. Michel?"

He hesitated before saying, "Because it's the right thing to do." But the words hadn't had time to settle before he was striding toward her. He didn't stop until he was inches away. He took her hands in his. "That's not the complete truth."

Leading her to a nearby settee, he silently urged her to sit. He eased himself down next to her.

Something extraordinary was about to take place. She could feel it in the air. Hope escalated, but reality quickly dashed it.

"Oh, Etienne..." Emotion lodged in her throat and she tugged her fingers free of his.

Fate was so cruel to fulfill her dreams only to steal them right away.

She forced herself to look into his eyes, the sadness she felt emanating from her in waves. "I can't let you do this. I have nothing to offer you, Etienne. Absolutely nothing."

He studied her silently for what seemed like minutes, but she knew must have been only seconds. Long, endless seconds.

"I came here all those months ago," he said quietly, reaching over and taking her hand in his once again, "in pursuit of a princess. A strong woman who could unite our families, our countries. I arrived here with nothing but that duty on my mind."

He oh-so-gently squeezed her fingers. "What I took as my royal obligation might have been what prompted our first meeting. But it was you who stole my heart. All those months ago when I came here to take you to the opera."

Her eyes rounded. "But I behaved abominably back then."

His mouth pulled into a grin that was wide and terribly sexy. "I know. And that's what clinched it for me. The fact that you slipped off…that you just couldn't resist escaping what you felt was a boring evening…that's what let me know that you were the one for me. I knew you'd always keep me guessing. You'd keep my life interesting. It was then I decided I had to have you."

She didn't know what to say. She couldn't believe the words he was speaking. Somehow, she just couldn't trust this was real.

Ariane swallowed. "But what about your parents? What about the duty you told me about? Your father will be furious—"

"Shhh," he said, pressing his fingertips gently

against her mouth. "My parents are quite happy to see me happy." He moistened his lips. "You see, the duty I felt pressured over was coming from me. I thought it was the thing I was supposed to do. My parents' marriage was a love match from the beginning. My mother and father fell in love, and their fate was sealed."

His brows drew together. "When you showed up in Rhineland acting as if you had noodles in your head, I was determined to discover what you were up to. When news of your—" He stopped short, seemingly unable to speak the one word that might bring her pain. His tone softened when he continued, "When news of your father's previous marriage came to light, all I could think of was protecting you. Even though I knew your situation had changed, it didn't change my feelings of wanting to be near you. And when we ran off for our day of fun and I saw that you were just as smart as I knew you were...it really didn't matter to me why you'd want to put on an act. All I knew was that I wanted you."

Intensity darkened his gaze. "I love you, Ariane. Please say you'll marry me."

Just then Jacqueline ran from where she'd evidently been eavesdropping. "A wedding! A wedding! We're having another wedding. Please, Ariane, please, please, please don't make me light candles. I want to be a bridesmaid. I'm old enough. I am!"

"Jacqueline de Bergeron, you little minx!" The regal Simone strode into the room. "Your sister hasn't even had a chance to accept the man's proposal."

Ariane saw the way her grandmother's eyes were shining with unadulterated joy so she didn't have the heart to point out that the elderly woman's obvious snooping just outside the door made her just as much a minx as Jacqueline.

Screwing up her face, Ariane asked Etienne, "You really want to unite yourself with this crazy family?"

In answer, Etienne got down on one knee. "I do."

Ariane's heart filled with love. "Then how can I possibly refuse you?"

Epilogue

As she stood in the doorway of the ancient stone church dressed in all this royal finery, Ariane had never felt more like a princess. Her grandmother's dress fit her to a T. Her hair had been coiffed and adorned with diamond-studded clips that glimmered from beneath the filmy veil.

The love of her life waited for her at the altar. Etienne looked mouth-wateringly handsome in his high-buttoned scarlet jacket and black trousers with razor-sharp creases. He looked eager...and nervous, as if he thought she might suddenly decide not to join him there to exchange vows of love and fidelity.

She smiled softly because she knew in her heart there was a greater chance that the whole of Rhineland would crumble and disappear than there was of her changing her mind about becoming his wife.

Forever and always.

She'd heard it said that a woman would never experience more anxiety than on the day she pledged herself to a man. But Ariane felt no butterflies in her stomach. All she experienced was a heady excitement that was nearly a fever of hope and love. She wanted to race up the aisle, shout her vows for all to hear and then fling herself into Etienne's arms. But she knew the dowager queen would be mortified by such behaviour, and that thought had Ariane suppressing the impish chuckle that threatened to bubble up from her throat.

The citizens of both St. Michel and Rhineland had been in an uproar when they'd discovered that she and her sisters had been stripped of their royal titles. But Ariane had suffered very little tumult from the ordeal. In fact, she'd delighted in the freedom that the circumstances had lent…even though those circumstances had been all too fleeting.

In marrying Etienne, the crown prince of Rhineland, Ariane would once again be an official princess with all the responsibilities and restrictions that came with the title. Did that bother her? Not in the least. Because the benefits of such a position outweighed the liabilities. By far.

The strains of the old pump organ filled the air of the tiny chapel—the only church in all of Rhineland that could accommodate this lightning-fast wedding of hers and Etienne's—and Georges stepped up beside her, offering her his arm.

"Are you ready?" her stepbrother asked softly. "Your groom awaits."

At that moment, she became aware of the exhilarated tension that seemed to pulsate from the wedding guests.

Offering Georges a bright smile, Ariane slid her hand over the crook of his proffered arm. "I'm more than ready. In fact, I'm counting on you to keep me from making a total fool of myself by sprinting up there to him."

Georges chuckled, cocking a brow at her. "That wouldn't be very ladylike, now would it?"

Ariane silently shook her head, and trained her gaze forward on the man with whom she would spend the rest of her life. His dove-gray eyes called to her, mesmerized her, lured her like the pulling and tugging of some irresistible magnetic energy.

Automatically, she tightened her grip on her step-brother's arm and forced her steps to remain slow and measured. She was determined to act in a manner befitting her position. Later there would be plenty of time to follow the urges of her heart.

How lucky she was, she thought, her heart pounding in breathless anticipation with each and every step she took closer to her future. How very, very lucky.

Hours later, it took the two of them many long and frustrating minutes to free Ariane from the yards and yards of Italian satin and French chiffon. There must have been a hundred tiny buttons needing to be unfastened. Etienne had taken his sweet time undoing them, following each and every one with a passionate kiss that had her panting for his touch.

Etienne's ceremonial garb was tossed hither and yon, the trousers over the back of the chair, jacket lying in a pile on the floor, while the shoes ...well, the whereabouts of his shoes was anyone's guess.

Finally the newly married couple were free of the constraints of clothing and were swathed in nothing more than the cool satin sheets of their honeymoon bed.

"Lord," Etienne groaned into Ariane's hair, "do you know how long I've yearned for this?"

She laughed. "I don't know what you're complaining about." She kissed one corner of his mouth. "I had to wait two whole weeks for this while I planned the wedding."

He grinned, kissing her back. "And it was a wonderful job you did, too."

Ariane lifted her arm, resting it on the pillow above her head. She sighed dreamily. "It was a nice wedding wasn't it? Jacqueline was a beautiful bridesmaid. So were Marie-Claire, Lise and Juliet. Georges was good enough to agree to walk me down the aisle, even though he just did the same for Marie-Claire two short weeks ago. Gosh, even Celeste was almost nice."

Etienne grimaced comically. "Almost."

Grinning, Ariane smoothed her fingers down her husband's jaw. "You've made my grandmother very happy."

"Oh?"

She nodded. "You married me for love," she told him. "That was very important to her...seeing her granddaughters marry for love rather than duty." A sexy chuckle bubbled up from her throat. "And the fact that you've promised to keep me in crème brûlé all the days of my life didn't hurt. She loves knowing I'll be well cared for."

Lowering his head, Etienne placed a hot kiss high on her milky breast. "Can we stop talking about your family? I didn't marry them. I married you. And I'm anxious to make you my wife...in every sense of the word."

"Mmmm." Ariane squirmed slowly until she positioned herself intimately beneath him. "I like that idea. Very much."

Happiness. Contentment. Ecstasy. Love to last a lifetime.

All the things she thought were lost to her, she'd found in her prince. Etienne was her soul mate. The man who made all her dreams come true.

And she would love him for all eternity.

* * * * *

Turn the page for a sneak preview
of the next
ROYALLY WED:
THE MISSING HEIR *title,*
A PRINCESS IN WAITING
Charles and Lise's story!
by Carol Grace
On sale in May 2002
in Silhouette Romance…
And don't miss any of the books
in the ROYALLY WED *series,*
only from Silhouette Romance:
OF ROYAL BLOOD
March 2002
by Carolyn Zane
IN PURSUIT OF A PRINCESS
April 2002
by Donna Clayton
A PRINCESS IN WAITING
May 2002
by Carol Grace
A PRINCE AT LAST!
June 2002
by Cathie Linz

Chapter One

Once upon a time in a small country called St. Michel, wedged between France and Rhineland, lived a beautiful princess named Lise de Bergeron. The princess didn't live in the stately palace with its turrets and ballroom and bevy of servants. She lived in a small cottage on the palace grounds. Lise had no crown and no legitimacy since her parents' marriage had been declared invalid. She was not surrounded by maids who waited on her hand and foot. She was attended by her former nanny, the woman who had raised her when her mother deserted her and her sisters. Nanny was old now and afflicted by arthritis and it was Princess Lise who was more caregiver then pampered princess.

A lack of royal trappings did not bother the princess. What did bother her was that her father the king had recently died, she'd been deserted by her husband, Wilhelm of neighboring Rhineland, and she was three months pregnant. All in all, this past year had been a difficult one. The future was unclear. What was in store for her and her unborn child?

Things had been worse when she was married to Wilhelm. Yes, they'd lived splendidly in Rhineland where he, as a member of the royal family, had money and power. But he was a cold, arrogant, ambitious man who'd been chosen for her by her father for political reasons. If she had one thing to be thankful for, it was that she was rid of the scoundrel. She'd endure any amount of shame if she never had to see him again.

An hour later she heard a car pull up in front of the cottage.

After a few moments, there was a knock on the door of the greenhouse. Lise pushed an errant strand of hair back from her face.

"Yes?"

"Lise?" It was a deep voice. Vaguely familiar. "It's Charles. Charles Rodin."

"Charles?" Charles, her husband's twin brother? What on earth was he doing here. Anything, anyone connected with her ex-husband was upsetting and an intrusion in her new life. Wilhelm had left her and she wanted no reminders of the biggest mistake of her life.

"Can I come in?" he asked.

As annoyed as she was, she couldn't help but notice the difference. Wilhelm would have barged in. His brother waited to be invited.

She opened the door. And stared at the man who stood there. He looked disturbingly like her ex-husband and yet the expression on his face was nothing like Wilhelm's arrogance. She barely remembered Charles from her wedding, at which he was the best man, and she hadn't seen him since that fateful day, but she knew this was a man who was self-confident but not arrogant. Still, the resemblance bothered her and brought back unpleasant memories. She wanted nothing to do with Wilhelm or any member of his family. She was doing her best to forget all of them. And now this…

"Can I come in?" he asked again.

What was wrong with her? She'd been raised with better manners than to let a guest stand in the doorway. But he was so big, so broad-shouldered, so startlingly like his brother, she thought he *was* in.

"Of course," she said briskly.

He stepped into the small greenhouse with the earthen floor and suddenly the glassed-in room was crowded to overflowing. She had no space, no room to breathe or think. There was a fluttery feeling in the pit of her stomach. She tried to think of something to say, but her mind was blank. All she could do was to stand there and wait for him to say something.

After a long silence during which he looked her up and down with a shade too much intimacy and she continued to stare at him, she finally found her voice.

"What is it, Charles, what do you want?"

He frowned at her lack of civility. What did he expect, that she'd welcome him with open arms, after what his brother did to her?

"I came when I heard the news, about the divorce…to see if…to see what I could do."

"Nothing. You can do nothing. You can't stop your brother from divorcing me, you can't make my parents' marriage valid, you can't find an heir for our country and you can't bring my father back to life.

So go back to your country and tell your brother I don't need him or his family."

Charles looked surprised at her angry words. "I haven't been in my country for months nor have I seen much of my family. Perhaps you aren't aware, but my brother and I have never been close. And now we are hardly on speaking terms," he said stiffly. "We lead separate lives, both professionally and personally. When I ran into Wilhelm last week in Los Angeles he told me about the divorce. I couldn't believe it. It's only been, what..."

"Eight months," Lise said. "Eight months that I am doing my best to forget. So if you don't mind, I'll get back to work." She pivoted on her heel and turned back to her frame. If only she'd been wearing a gown and a tiara, she might have pulled off this obvious dismissal and he would have left. She'd used the imperial tone. She had the movement down pat. Those years of training in demeanor came in useful at times. But not today. He didn't leave. He did just the opposite. He stepped forward. He was right behind her, leaning over her left shoulder.

She wasn't quite sure what to make of him. Or why he was there in the first place. She didn't know how to get rid of him. Or if she really wanted to. There were questions she wanted answers to. And she had to admit she wanted to know how Charles felt about her.

Charles leaned back against a stone countertop and studied her for a long moment. He was trying to collect his thoughts, but just looking at the lovely princess caused his mind to wander and his heart to pound erratically. The last time he'd seen Lise de Bergeron had been on her wedding day.

He'd thought at that time that in her white satin gown and diamond tiara she was the most beautiful thing he'd ever seen. He'd been filled with an unbecoming rush of envy for his older brother. As usual, Wilhelm had succeeded in snatching the prize before Charles had a chance to compete.

When his brother found out Lise was illegitimate and would inherit nothing, he immediately divorced her. When Charles heard that straight from his brother's mouth he was stunned. His brother was not known for his kindness or compassion, he'd always had a ruthless streak, pushing aside anyone and anything that got in his way, but this time he'd gone too far. Charles was not only stunned, but he was ashamed on behalf of the family honor. He was determined to do something to make things right.

She didn't know why he was there, but he did. He'd planned his speech. He knew what he had to say, but now that he was there and she was looking at him with those incredible blue eyes, he could only stand and stare.

She'd changed. It had only been eight months, but she was not the same demure princess who'd dazzled him on her wedding day. It wasn't only her clothing, it was her manner. He thought she'd be meek and mild and jump at the chance he was going to offer her. Now he wasn't so sure. She had a stubborn tilt to her chin, a proud look in her eyes and a certain tone to her voice. If he'd been infatuated with her before, he was fascinated now. He didn't know what she was going to say next. He decided to put off his declaration.

"I mustn't keep you any longer, Charles," she

said, glancing at the door. It was plain she was dismissing him before he'd said what he'd come to say.

He'd hoped to establish a mood and set up the appropriate atmosphere. He'd planned to lead up to it gradually, but he no longer had time. It was clear it had to be now. He stood and looked down at her. It was now or never. He took a deep breath.

"I came today to offer my hand in marriage," he said.